# The Trial of the Gods

Khonani Ontebetse

First Edition: June 2011; updated December 2011
Published by Nsemia Inc. Publishers (www.nsemia.com)


Edited By: Sarah Kibaalya
Cover Concept Illustration: Abel Murumba
Cover Design: Danielle Pitt
Layout Design: Kemunto Matunda

Note for Librarians:
A cataloguing record for this book is available from
Library and Archives Canada.



ISBN: 978-1-926906-07-2 Paperback

*To the Dispossessed*

# Acknowledgements

I would like to thank the following for helping me to make this work a success: Olopeng Rabasimane, Bonani Monnagaetsho, and Leisure Mmolawa. I am grateful for parents Teezdani Ontebetse and Ontebetse Majatsie, and the many others (who I cannot all name) that expressed con¬fidence in this novel.

# About the Author

Khonani Ontebetse was born in Zoroga, Botswana in 1978. He was educated at Masunga Senior Secondary School and Nelson Mandela Metropolitan University (NMMU). After receiving a Bachelor of Arts degree in Media Communication and Culture at NMMU in 2005, Khonani worked as a journalist for **The Ngami Times** newspaper and later **The Mirror** newspaper. He is currently a journalist for *The Botswana Gazette.*

In 2004, when the then Port Elizabeth University and Port Elizabeth Technikon merged to form the NMMU, Khonani was among the four students from the two institutions to win a literary competition with his essay entitled- ***"How I will remember The University of Port Elizabeth."*** That was the turning point in his career as an ambitious writer.

In 2008, he won the first Bessie Head Literature Awards, a locally-run literary competition in Botswana for his novel titled *Born with a Husband* (Pentagon Publishers) Bessie Head Literature Awards are held annually in honour of one Africa's acclaimed writers, the late Bessie Head. *Born with a Husband* discusses arranged marriages in relation to HIV/AIDS. Khonani's other works are short stories and plays which are yet to be published.

# Foreword

This is a book not to be forgotten as it will always remind us of what is happening today. Its author Khonani Ontebetse has reconstructed a story that can change the understanding not just of Africa, but of the world in general.

Who would have thought that in Africa today we still need to be reminded that "the governing race is first and foremost those who come from elsewhere, those who are unlike the original inhabitants, "the others."

The novel's description of the events as they unfold recalls Frantz Fanon's *The Wretched of The Earth.* The notion that blacks in Africa are expected to treat each other as one of their own despite their ethnic differences is explored in this book. In fact the novel, as some have observed before, unravels a leap of understanding that has to be made before people can really come to terms with the fact that the Basarwa are not considered black by black Africans -they're considered to be inferior with some leaders in the continent calling them backward creatures.

While *The Trial of The Gods* is also a heartfelt journey into the recent trials and tribulations of Basarwa (Bushmen), it is also an accurate portrayal of the basic human endeavour - belonging. Belonging is the most important theme in this novel and the author's intimacy with his subjects lends awesome credibility to the tale; told through the eyes of a homesick elder. The author takes the reader through an unforgettable account of the unravelling of the Botswana Government's treatment of one of its own vulnerable members in the society, the down trodden, the dispossessed.

*The Trial Of the Gods* is a must read for anyone seeking understanding into the most primal of human desires, understanding of the connection between land and identity as well as the development challenges of Africa.

But who would have also thought that Botswana, with its tag of a shining example of Africa and a country that prides itself on being a modern nation could treat some of its citizens with an iron fist in pursuit of earthly riches? It is through the *The Trial of the Gods* that the question whether the country has shown signs of losing a grip on some key governance attribute comes under the spotlight. Is it true that Botswana is a shining example of democracy in Africa and enjoys socioeconomic stability than other countries in the African continent? Or is this propaganda, a false, vigorously promoted by multinational companies and Europe and their local home guards because they want to benefit from the Southern African countries' rich diamonds? Those are some the questions that are raised in the book. In summary, the author has successfully explored and done justice to the treatment of the theme of human ideals.

# Chapter One

Today all the representatives of the First People of Kalahari (FPK) organization were gathered at the leader of the organization's home in Ghanzi. The letter was addressed to the leaders of FPK. Keoreng Molefe, coordinator and secretary of the organization looked at the leader of FPK.

"We are here to see the letter, Jay." He surveyed the men who were present with his eyes to show and confirm that indeed he was speaking on their behalf.

"We believe that you are the person who received it." Molefe stole a quick glance at Jay. He then looked at the hearth. There was a dying log near where Jay sat; most of the logs on the other side had stopped smouldering. Near a tripod, lay firewood of all sizes.

"That is true," said Jay, also surveying the FPK leaders. His companion of all times, Jamana was among them. There was a look of surprise on Jamana's face, which he failed to conceal. But apart from Jay, the others failed to detect this as they were facing the same direction as Jamana.

Molefe's face lit with a smile that could have been joy or surprise.

"It is true that greetings from a friend are like a medicine." Unexpectedly, the smile melted into a nervous grin. "We cannot just ignore those who want to assist us."

"Who told you about it?" Jay asked looking beyond his listeners' heads, into the endless Kalahari Desert plains.

"It is not a matter of who told us," Molefe said his voice raised and his neck inclined to one side.

"Did you or did you not receive the letter is all we would like to know. Don't tell us that so-and-so knows about it. What we would like to see is the contents of the letter."

Jamana smiled again but said nothing. Jay bowed his head. "Why do you care about letters and court application papers?"

He nearly smiled as well.

"Is the court application not lying in those magnificent court buildings the one delaying us from going back home?"

Jamana raised his head from the hearth and looked at Jay. "But let's see the letter." Suddenly his smile faded into a wrinkled face. "A court process normally takes longer than expected, Jay."

"We cannot wait to go back home," Jay said, not showing any sign that he would produce the letter. There was silence.

"Jay," said Molefe in a serious voice than before. "We have been working together as an organization on a number of issues since the strange pestilence that struck our people when they were forced to relocate from the place given to us by the Gods. We have also worked with Survival International in an effort to show those who want to relocate our people that when they came here to live before independence from Britain, the land belonged to us. Now they are fighting us for a land that belongs to us. And you Jay, you know this very well. But why are you giving us trouble regarding this letter from the same organization that wants to correct the wrong that even the ancestors of those who want to move us out of our homes can see from their resting place?" No one spoke. Jay shook his head as if responding to a question inside his head.

"Lorato," he called out. A voice of a young girl answered from one of the huts adjacent to the one whose shade they were sitting under.

"Tell your mother to give you a black book sandwiched between the rafters and the thatch. Then bring it here," he said.

"Mother has gone to draw water from the stream," Lorato said from the same hut.

"Ask your young mother then," Jay said referring to his other young wife. Then there was silence again, tension followed. It was broken by Lorato who greeted in the customary manner by kneeling down. She handed over the book to her father and paused for further instructions, her thumb in her mouth.

"It is okay," Jay said to his daughter. "You may go."

Jay examined the threads that wrapped the book, found the knot and unfastened it, placing the book on his lap as he did so. The four visitors were looking at him with revived interest. Jay sorted out the letters sandwiched between the pages of the book like a post officer. He took out a letter with a British stamp and handed it over to Jamana. But the other man shook his head, and pointed at Molefe. Molefe's eyes lit up upon meeting the contents of the letter causing Jamana and the others to peer at the document.

"Would you please read it," he said handing it over to Jamana.

"Jay, why have you been keeping this as a secret?" Jamana asked without reading the letter. Then Jamana began to read the first passage of the letter.

*"We as Survival International are the friends of oppressed people all over the world."* He nodded and nearly whistled to himself. Then he continued; *"We are going to ensure that the eviction of the Basarwa in Botswana from their ancestral land will be known by everyone all over the world. People, even those in Africa, should know that we represent people not on the basis of their religion, race, ethnicity or nationality. We don't have boundaries. We are an organization that knows no borders when it comes to issues of human rights, especially rights that concern minority groups.*

*"For instance we have helped the Aborigines in Australia,*

*the native Indians in South America, just to mention a few. We don't care if we are criticized by governments or other Non Governmental Organizations (NGOs). We have been criticized before and we know how to handle criticism. We know what minority groups want. We understand their ways and their lifestyle. We do not discriminate.*

*"Discrimination is what we are fighting against. And we are unstoppable. Even our people here in Britain criticize our work, but we ensure that the oppressed get unprecedented coverage and help. Normally, we have an audience with Members of parliament here in Britain when they complain.*

*"For instance, we have just briefed them on the situation of the Basarwa in one of their former colonies, Bechuanaland, which is now called Botswana or the Switzerland of Africa, as it is called by those who admire it.*

*"We even sacrifice our lives when it comes to human rights issues. Was not one of our researchers killed by the South African apartheid lunatics in 1988? We, liberals and human rights activists, are always at the receiving end. Even from people who are considered civilized like some of our friends in South Africa. Another issue that we nearly forgot is that we have also been following the local NGOs who are trying to help the Basarwa. We are of the view that these NGOs are the biggest liars to our friends, the Basarwa. In fact they are the Basarwa's enemies. For the Basarwa to agree to be helped by these NGOs would be like sleeping with an enemy. If indeed local NGOs knew anything about relocations, there would never have been any in the first place. They would have nipped the problem in the bud..."*

After he had read the letter, Jamana looked at Jay once again. In fact, all eyes were on Jay now. Jay felt like running away from them. He did not know who to believe.

The negotiation team, which included local NGOs such as Ditshwanelo, Kuru Development Trust, WIMSA? Or now Survival International which was now saying these organizations had in fact promised lies?

"What do you want me to do?" he asked, his eyes vaguely surveying the hearth.

"We should be asking you that question," said Aron, who had not said anything since the meeting began.

Jay sighed hard, shook his head and rolled his eyes from the hearth trying to find a different object on which to concentrate. Suddenly he broke into a series of quiet coughs.

"We are not saying you should give us the answer now," said Molefe without emotion. Turning his eyes from Jay to Aron he added: "But remember that people want to go back home as soon as possible." There was a murmur of approval from the other men.

Jay rubbed his nose with the back of his hand.

"That is what everybody wants," he said raising his head a little, his voice not louder than a whisper. "But now I'm confused. I don't know who to trust."

"Perhaps if we leave you alone," Jamana said, "the confusion will clear from your head the same way a beer clears from a drunken man's head the following day."

Jay frowned like a man waking up from a bad dream.

"Whether we will get back the land Jamana, and how, is what I would like to know!"

Jamana again unfurled the letter from Survival International and glanced at its contents. He looked at Jay with narrow eyes that were neither optimistic nor pessimistic.

"They say, this is not our piece of land, Jay," he said looking away. His eyes filled with tears that could have made channels in the Kalahari Desert. And without attempting to rub away the teardrops he added; "that is why we need

Survival international. Let's prepare for the journey to court tomorrow. We will find out from the Court who the real owner of the land is. We expect a British lawyer to arrive in Gaborone anytime from now."

The other men nodded as each of them rose, each dusting his behind with the palm of his hand. Jay only shrugged and bowed his head as the four men walked away and left him alone.

# Chapter Two

The Lobatse High court, roughly 70 kilometres from the capital city of Gaborone, is decorated with attractive hardwood panelling inside. Glass separates the counsels' table from the raised public gallery with walls made of beautifully shaped stones. There are three prominent seats at the same level as those occupied by the public. While the seats for the judges and the public are a little bit raised, those for the counsels are lowered so that the judges and the public appear dominant. The Central Kalahari Game Reserve (CKGR) case was now before the High Court of three judges comprising Matlotla Ditiro, Antoinette Brown and Pamaniwa Pamani.

The lead applicant in the case was Jay. A lawyer from Britain had just filed a legal appearance form confirming that he would represent Jay and his people.

Accompanying the lawyer was a local instructing attorney. The state was represented by a top Government attorney, a man who was well acquainted with constitutional rights. The battle for the soul of the Kalahari Desert, the GKGR, and its invisible inhabitants had begun. And Jay was one of those invisible residents.

A constable walked through the court room doors, returning almost at once. There was a loud bang and the three judges walked in donning their black robes.

"My Lords," said the British lawyer as soon as Judge Ditiro had focused his eyes on him.

"My names are Garden Benny..." He paused as the three judges jotted down his names.

"I will be representing Mr. Jay Setlhare and the other

241 applicants all former residents of the Central Kalahari Game Reserve or CKGR, and accompanying me is the instructing attorney, Mr. Dumelang Phoko." He sat down.

"I'm Saede Peolwane," said the State lawyer getting up. "I represent the State in this matter," turning his head with a mischievous smile he added, "and with me is Mr. Dintwa Molao who will be assisting me." Then he sat down.

"Mr. Benny," said Judge Brown. "Have you replaced the advocates from South Africa in this matter?"

"Yes My Lady. I was under the impression that my colleague had already informed the court about this latest development."

Judge Brown nodded and said the court had only just learnt about the change. Benny took his spectacles off and ran his tongue across his lips.

"My Lords, there is no need for this court to relocate to CKGR. I pray that the issue of going to Gope in CKGR for inspection be struck off." As Benny addressed the court in English, an interpreter would translate this into one of the national languages, Setswana.

Judge Ditiro raised his eyes from a pile of papers before him. He now fixed his eyes on Saede Peolwane.

"We would like to raise an objection to that," said Peolwane, "because we would like to clear any doubt that the world may have." He paused and perused the files on the table before him.

"The first applicant Mr. Jay Setlhare and Survival International have made serious allegations that the relocation is linked to diamonds. Mr. Setlhare has said this in the newspapers many times. These are serious allegations that should not be left unchallenged. We are not apologetic about whether there are any mining activities going on there because that is the government's policy. In addition to that, at the end of the day the minerals are going to benefit every citizen. But we have a problem when such claims are made and not substantiated." Peolwane sat down. Judge Ditiro nodded his head towards Benny.

"I ask this court to take into consideration the problems and challenges faced by my clients," said Benny. "They are as Frantz Fanon, the Algerian/French philosopher would put it, *The Wretched Of the earth*. We do not have money for the trip to CKGR..." Judge Ditiro's rough voice interrupted Benny.

"Yes Mr. Benny," said the Judge with a smile as if amused by Benny's reference to Frantz Fanon. "That is a very interesting observation you have just made there. But I would Like to draw your attention to the argument raised by Mr. Peolwane that there have been letters in the press written by Mr. Setlhare to the effect that there are mining activities in CKGR. And perhaps you should also address another serious allegation, as Mr. Peolwane put it, that the first applicant said he had no confidence in court proceedings." Benny rose to his feet reluctantly as if his reputation and experience as a human rights lawyer in a number of African and other countries was being challenged.

"My Lords." Benny pulled at his long robes as if for advice. "My clients are not part of those allegations. They have never said anything about mining in CKGR. In fact they are not part of the campaign that says people were relocated because of mining or diamonds. I would advise Mr. Setlhare to see to it that he tells the world that there are no mining activities in CKGR. For the record, we have no claims of mining activities in our application. Our main issue is that the applicants should be allowed to go back home. The constitution should recognize that my applicants have rights." Judge Ditiro glanced at Peolwane.

"Mr. Peolwane," he called out. "What do you have to say to that?"

"The applicants might have arrived early in Southern

Africa," said Peolwane. "But that does not give them the right to be lawless in a liberal society. They cannot demand that they do as they please." He glanced at the three judges and then at Benny before he sat down. Peolwane could have made Adolf Hitler and Goebbels proud, Benny reflected as he glanced at the top State lawyer, while rising to his feet.

"My Lords."' Benny never addressed the court without, "My Lord." In his thirty  years of experience he had learnt that this had the effect of drawing the attention of the judges, convince them effectively.

"We would like to bring a number of witnesses later but for now we will only wait to hear the evidence of state witnesses."

0-0-0-0-0

The first witness to take the witness box was Thata Mojuta, the former District Commissioner of Ghanzi, under whose district the disputed ancestral land fell.

"Mr. Mojuta, tell this court what you know," said Peolwane after a formal introduction of the witness.

Mojuta wet his lips. He scratched his head like a beautiful girl from a poor family being proposed to by a rich old man.

"We registered people," he said. He crossed his hands at his back. "These were people who wanted to relocate."

"Did they tell you that they wanted to move out?"

"Yes they did." He clenched his hands and put them on the stand before him, next to a Bible which he had used to take an oath. "They were willing to move out, yes."

Peolwane turned his eyes from the witness to the judges.

"That is all I wanted to ask the witness."

"Yes Mr. Benny," said Judge Ditiro. Benny rose to his feet and strode toward the witness.

"Mr. Mojuta."

In response Mojuta raised his eyebrows. Benny nodded his head twice as if he and Mojuta shared a juicy secret that would make headlines in The Voice newspaper. "You said the people were willing to move?"

"Yes."

"How did you know?"

"Because some of them told me that..."

"They...ok finish your sentence."

"That their livestock was in danger of wild animals."

"If those people were to be paraded before this court would you recognize or identify them?"

"No."

"And you want this court to believe your story?"

"Yes."

"Mr. Mojuta, I'm going to tell this court that there is nothing that suggests truth in your evidence." Mojuta took away his hands from the table. He wanted to cross them behind him, but instead folded them across his chest, before letting them fall to his sides. His eyes were shining as if he had seen a large snake, such as the one he once saw crossing a path when he visited the CKGR for the first time.

"Why should this court believe your story?"

"Because...Because...Because."

Mojuta seemed to have difficulties in choosing words though he was speaking his home language, Setswana. Earlier Benny had requested that the court proceedings be conducted in English only but the Judges said English and Setswana were national languages, hence they were admissible in court. An interpreter was called. Mojuta shifted his gaze from Benny who was an arm's length away from him to the three judges as if in appeal. The trick worked.

"Because when I took the oath before giving evidence this morning I said I was going to tell this court nothing but the truth."

"But Mr. Mojuta if you are telling the truth how can you forget to recognize people that you were dealing with? It goes to show that you are not telling the truth." Peolwane shot up. "Objection! The witness never…"

"Objection overruled," responded Judge Ditiro.

Benny nodded his head as if thanking the Judge. He looked at Mojuta.

"How many people did you register in each settlement in CKGR?"

"I can't remember, but there were not many."

"My Lord, that is all," said Benny with his hands crossed behind his back and moving away from the witness. Peolwane rose to his feet. Judge Ditiro nodded.

"Yes Mr. Peolwane, what is it that you want?"

"We will call other witnesses during the next court session. However, we would like to let the court know that we are concerned," said Peolwane. "We are concerned that Jay and Jamana continue to take the law into their own hands by going back inside the reserve. By doing so they are even undermining the authority of the court. They had been compensated after the relocation. So we seek protection from the court."

"My Lord," said Benny rising. "My clients are impatient to be with their ancestors because I'm told they get protection from them according to their culture." He paused and turning his head, strained his ear toward the instructing attorney, Dumelang Phoko. Benny glanced at the three judges, his eyes narrowing.

"My Lords, I wish to stop here. There is a new development. I'm advised that we may withdraw the case because we have no funds."

Judge Brown fixed her eyes on Benny, and for a moment they were immobile.

"But Mr. Benny, a lawyer can handle a case for a minimum fee."

The British lawyer nodded as if he was faced with a judicial fact that he could not deny. He strengthened up his arched back and crossed his hands behind his back.

"Yes My Lady," Benny agreed with Judge Brown. "But we have never considered other means. May I consult with my clients for a minute?"

Judge Brown nodded and forced a smile.

"Yes Sir."

Benny walked to where Jay was sitting with Jamana. For the first time in his thirty-year career, he was representing a principal applicant wearing traditional decorative horns in court! Not even in other African countries he had been to. Apart from the horns, Jay wore a fur jacket made from the hide of an antelope. He also wore headgear decorated with beads and an amulet from a steenbok. He looked up as soon as Benny whispered something into Jamana's ears. Jay stole a quick glance at the lawyer, and focused his eyes on the three judges who, in his eyes, were like aliens from another planet.

Jay sighed, echoing the silence of his people in the Kalahari Desert. He shook his head as if he was talking to his personal god.

"I will have to be asked questions in the CKGR," he said, "so that the ancestors can give me instructions on what to say." Jay said this louder than necessary despite Benny admonishing him to tone it down. The lawyer tried to hush Jay as one would a crying baby whose toy has been

13

snatched away by a stranger. Perhaps the CKGR was that special toy. Strangers, as prophesied by the ancestors, were coming from all over the world to take away his land and he did not want to lose it. Jay would not hear the lawyer's advice and warded off Benny's bony hands, as they sought to calm him down. For a moment the lawyer and the client looked as if they would come to blows. Benny folded his arms across his chest as if protecting it from an expected blow from Jay's fists. Unexpectedly, Jay took his eyes off Benny and focused them on the three judges. When he spoke, his voice was hoarse and louder than before. It was as if he was now the judge and the three judges were uncooperative accused persons.

"The ancestors have to tell me whether to move out of our home or not. Unless I get permission or advice from the ancestors who are my parents, there is no way I can help this court. This is because in our culture a son does not do anything without permission from his parents. It is a deadly sin to do so, and you are asking me to confront death."

Benny did not understand. "If you want to give evidence wait until you take the oath."

Jay looked at Jamana and shook his head. Jamana said nothing or he had nothing to say. "At least, do not give interviews to newspapers," Benny said as he walked away from Jamana and Jay toward the counsels' tables.

Unexpectedly again, Jay stood up at the same time.

"I still have to consult with my clients," said Benny. "There are a number of issues that we need to iron out."

With these words he looked towards Jay again, but was only able to catch a glimpse of an antelope fur jacket closing the court room doors, its owner shutting himself off from the case and court proceedings. Benny thought the scene mirrored the manner in which the CKGR had been shut off from the outside world before diamond explorers, tourists, politicians, human rights organizations and the media started to develop interest in it.

Judge Pamani raised an eyebrow and whispered to Judge Ditiro and then to Judge Brown. "Mr. Benny, it appears your clients are eager to have this case held in their ancestral land as the lead applicant Mr. Setlhare has suggested. Never before have we heard of a man who cannot speak unless he gets advice from his ancestors. Anyway, the court will respect your clients' wishes."

A mischievous smile danced on Judge Pamani's face as he continued with raised eyes. "Perhaps there will be no need for you to represent the applicants while they are in the CKGR as they will be getting instructions from the gods."

Benny giggled and the courtroom smiled at the judge's statement.

"Perhaps my service will no longer be needed when we are in CKGR. As you say My Lord," said Benny. "I will make an informed decision after I consult with my clients." The British lawyer sat down.

Judge Ditiro's lips parted slightly. "The matter has been postponed to May 14th," he said. "I hope those dates are suitable for all the learned counsels." Benny and Peolwane stood up simultaneously and voiced their agreement.

The courtroom cleared as soon as the judges had disappeared into their chambers.

0-0-0-0-0

Outside, Jay's reputation was taking a beating as people learnt that his lawyer had barred him from speaking to the newspapers. People wanted to read his interviews in newspapers; they wanted to see him on TV. That he could not speak to the papers was a great blow to his people who had no voice; no words of their own.

But his reputation recovered with reports that he was refusing to give evidence before a court of law. Further consolation came as news spread that Jay wanted his ancestors to instruct him as to what he should tell the court, and not his lawyers. He appeared to be looming large and beyond the knowledge of the judges, lawyers, newspapers and politicians. But how could a man refuse to give evidence before the Lobatse High Court in a case in which he was the principal applicant?

Never before had a man disrespected the authority of the court and also escaped being found guilty of contempt of court. But that was Jay. It appeared he was always beyond understanding. He appeared to be protected by an invisible hand, something out of the ordinary. Ironically, it was the state lawyer, Peolwane, instead who found himself locked up for contempt of court.

# Chapter Three

Outside the Lobatse High Court, after walking out in protest, Jay drew so hard on the cigarette that the smoke from his mouth and nostrils resembled the Blue Train charging its way from Francistown to Gaborone. Tossing the cigarette stub away, Jay saw Jamana's van pulling up from the parking bay in front of him. Jay walked towards the van's door, climbed in and slammed it shut behind him. Jamana could sense the utter hopelessness written on Jay's face. Jamana climbed out of the van and stood by the passenger door to talk to Jay.

"Let's have a word with the lawyers," he told Jay in Sesarwa.

But thinking about the CKGR and his people made Jay shake his head. He slumped on the seat and drew on another cigarette harder than before. In his mind he believed the leaders viewed his people as things, not humans. He found himself weeping, almost sobbing, recalling the terror and grief etched on his people's haunted faces. Not long ago, Jay had never thought such a disaster could befall his people.

"There is no need to," he said absentmindedly, his thoughts still on the events leading to his people looking for protection from the courts against the police's rubber bullets. "We have reached the end of the road; it is better we seek help from the gods," he said. Jamana did not respond quickly. Jay's words seemed to make him speechless.

"Why are the leaders of this country doing this to us Jamana, I can't understand?" he asked, turning his face away from Jamana as if pleading to the absent faces of the gods he spoke of.

"But what Benny, Phoko and Survival International

are doing has helped us, otherwise we would have been destroyed," Jamana replied at last, looking Jay in the eye while a sob choked his throat. Jay shrugged his shoulders, while Jamana shook his head and walked away to meet Benny and Phoko, a long look of uncertainty on his face. This gave Jay enough time to recall events that led to the circumstances that he and his people found themselves in.

0-0-0-0-0

Jay would always remember the Ghanzi District Council trucks with their logos on both front doors. The logos had a hunter holding a bow and arrow, flanked by an eland. Those were the trucks which were later piled high with thatched grass and long poles when the residents were relocated. For Jay, it was a day he would always remember. On that day, as he arrived from a long hunting trip, his fears and suspicions grew. The inevitable smoke was absent from the thatched huts of his three wives. However, he thought, that could have been a sign that they were preparing for his arrival, to get ready for supper. In fact, to get ready for a feast.

Was he not carrying the eland meat that they loved so much? This was the very meat they had been missing since he had been preoccupied with trips to Europe and the USA, during which he asked the world to help his people resist development and civilization, so the reports said.

It would be a lie for Jay to say he had not heard about the relocation. He had. He knew that from seven other settlements within the reserve such as Mothomelo, Gugama, Metsimanong and others.

He was also aware of the saying that the burning hut starts a fire on adjacent ones. So his place, his home, Molapo, was the next! But he never thought it could happen to his family or to his people in general. Relocation. That was for people in Mogoditshane or Tsolamosese. Those were settlements in Gaborone. Not here in the heart of

Kalahari Desert. But it seemed, or he realized later that the relocation from other settlements within the reserve had caught up with him.

His family obeyed him, this he was sure of. They could not disobey him. They could not move out of their home without his consent. But as he approached the homestead that day, the fear and suspicion made him quicken his steps. Jay refused to believe his eyes even as the evidence lay before him. Why didn't his children come out to welcome him? Had one of his dogs not arrived early, before him to announce his arrival?

And they should have known from its bulging stomach that his long day at the hunting expedition had not been in vain. The gods had answered his prayers after he had asked them to give him something, anything, during the trance dance. But his children did not shout to announce his arrival to their mothers. They should have met him on the way, to help him carry the eland meat. They did not.

Perhaps, Jay thought, he was still far from home and not close enough to be met yet. But when he was a few yards away his doubts distilled into fear. Suddenly, he was dumbstruck. Creases etched themselves on Jay's face and he shielded his eyes from the sun's rays. He peered carefully at what was supposed to have been his huts, his home. But there were no standing huts, no pots and no clothing hanging from the rafters of the huts. No chicken looking for worms in the grass. No animal kraal, no donkeys, no women carrying firewood. Where was that other hut which he had left full of melons and wild tubers that morning? Even the huts which were still under construction were not in sight. Jay was met only by a sealed borehole with no pump house. His lower jaw fell as it always did when he lost hope. He placed his hand over his open mouth in sheer amazement. The upright sticks around which had stood an old fence to protect his family from lions were gone.

There were no poles strung together with wires. Because there was nothing to protect now? Where was his family? Jay rubbed mud on his tyre-made sandals which had stuck when he had crossed the shallow water at the Kikaoi pans to reach a herd of drinking elands.

Perhaps his family had moved to another place within the reserve. Perhaps there had been an order from the gods to move. He looked at the homestead area. Once again he shook his head in disbelief. It could not be true.

Jay's three round thatched huts which belonged to his three wives were gone.

The huts had been demolished! Even the tree branch-made doors which lay vertically across the doors of the huts had been destroyed. He picked up the pieces of the doors and rafters and stroked them for a moment with his hands hoping they would reveal more about what happened. But they were silent. Indeed the huts had been ravaged, his home vandalized. No chicken roamed around, he reflected again with bitterness. His dogs groaned and climbed over his patched green overalls. They wagged their tails. It was as if they were searching for answers. In response, Jay brushed them aside and for a moment his anger was directed at them, and he whipped one of them called Tau.

Still smarting from the anger, he tried to draw water from the stand pipe to quench his thirst and dry throat. Nothing came out. The thirst had made Jay forget that the sealed bore hole with no pump house was the first sign he had seen that something was wrong. And he was really thirsty! And even more baffled. Then Jay understood. The bore hole where the standpipe tapped water from, had been cut off too. He examined the sandy soil carefully like a geologist surveying diamonds. There were also traces of boots and some footprints which he recognized as belonging to his wives and children. He peered once more as if he wanted to touch the traces to clear any doubt. He could tell from the traces of doves, insects and millipedes which had treaded on those of the trucks, boots and his family's footprints, that the people had left in the morning. He did not look at the ruins twice. He followed the marks left by the trucks heading southwards. His dogs ran after him. In his current state of mind, Jay did not, could not even see the fresh spoor of a lion that had just crossed the main path. In fact the lion strode elegantly toward the shade of a mosu tree. But Jay felt and saw nothing. All the thoughts that had been there during the hunting expedition had dissipated. He no longer thought of taking herbs to Ghanzi to cure patients. He did not want to think of how he would heal so-and-so. Or how he had expected to be happy to find one of his three wives making beads from ostrich eggs. Or making jewellery from porcupine quills and perhaps one of them preparing to cook fresh eland meat not the sliver of meat he had left hanging from rafters in the senior wife's hut. Jay's mind was on the task at hand, the mission to find his family and his people. Even the tsamma melon he had held in his hand fell to the ground. The eland meat dangling, hanging from a stick, on his shoulder had tumbled and fell in the sandy soil.

As he ran, it occurred to him that his family was the only one left in Molapo settlement. The relocation! Not so soon, Jay muttered still unable to believe that the family had been relocated. "From now on," he remembered warning his senior wife a few months earlier, "you should quit your job." Xhwaashe had not understood the sudden change in her husband. She was part of those employed at the Metsimanong settlement to carry out the relocation exercise.

"Why Jay?" she had raised her eyes at her husband in sheer amazement, but in a submissive voice. Xhwaashe had called her husband by his name without realizing it. She was supposed to call him "the father of my children" as was the custom; a mother was supposed to protect the culture.

"I say you should, at once," Jay said. "Or are you diabolically inspired by this talk of developments and civilization?" She went quiet. She knew that he meant what he said. She had to obey. In fact, she wept. She did not understand.

"I can see now that there is someone," he said, "where you have been hired that gave you leave to call me by my name. But the day will come that you will know who the head of the family is. It is not for you to behave like town women who are responsible for the break down of families and laid down morals because of their talk of equality."

Jay now set his eyes on the sandy paths running parallel to each other. He nearly collided with a car going toward the reserve and jumped into the bush. His dogs were still behind him. The tourists, amazed, laughed at him instead of being angry.

He had no time to reflect on this, though he also found it strange. What were they laughing at?

The journey was a long one without a proper road. He slung his bow across his back and held the arrows in his left hand still muttering inaudible words. By the time he joined a small path from Gugama, another settlement where people had been relocated from some few months ago, his overalls from the South African mines were torn to shreds by the shrubs. But Jay did not care. He felt nothing. He had to locate his family and then all his people. It was clear now that the people had been taken outside the reserve - their home. He had to find out who took them away from their huts and why. It was dawn when he reached his destination.

# Chapter Four

Jay looked at the new settlement; the shops, the houses, the clinic and the community bar. Everything summed up something he disliked, something he felt bitter about in two words: development and civilization. Jay could not believe that with these things before him - this civilization, this development - he had lost his home. Home being the CKGR, the ancestral land. Indeed that land was what he could call his people's property. The ancestral land, was it not a heritage, the protector of his culture and tradition? Hot saliva choked him. Jay knew from the voices of some residents who had not seen him, that with their talk of compensation which included cattle and money, the heritage had been sold. Suddenly, he hated his people, and those who had loaded them in the trucks and ferried them to this new place. He slumped on a stool near a baobab. A few people had gathered now.

"Lere," he called out in a detached voice, after a while the sound barely above a whisper.

"What is happening?"

Jay looked around shaking his head, and his eyes landed on a church building, children in school uniforms, and a water reservoir. There was a kgotla, customary court, made of a concrete structure and roofed with corrugated iron. His eyes also surveyed a clinic, a rural centre, an unused tannery, a primary school consisting of four buildings. Other buildings were still under construction, vendor shops, and a few huts were also under construction, he observed. So this was development and civilization?

"Lere what has happened?"

Lere was sitting opposite Jay. The old man's eyes were like a fog when he realized that still he had not answered even a single question from Jay. He rubbed them with the back of his eyes and sneezed.

"The ancestral land has been sold," said Lere attempting to rise. He placed his hand on his arched back, to straighten it up. His arms arched inwards, he supported his half erect position with a walking stick.

Lere's eyes were immobile, perhaps the only part of his craggy face that showed emotion.

"We believed them." Suddenly the eyes blinked and his breath was hard.

"We believed them when they said you are the very man who held negotiations with some men whose names are an offence to mention. They said you and other members of our organization, FPK, agreed that we should relocate... that you said the CKGR does not belong to us any more, fear hovered over our heads like..."

"I can't understand." Jay looked at the new settlement, the schools, clinics, and the community hall trying to grasp the meaning of relocation, of development and civilization. Perhaps these buildings could help him understand the meaning of what Lere was trying to explain.

"A snake is not pursued into its hole. What did you do when men came and stole our wives and children?"

Old man Lere sobbed as his mind recalled painful events during the relocation. He felt the pain of a son and the generation to come. "They came with trucks." He inclined on the walking stick, made of a branch, which supported his stooping back.

A teardrop fell. It was as if words caused him pain, visited his mind with violence. "Just as you and the others had left for hunting," he said, still wiping at his moist eyes, "they came and loaded your wives. We could see from their faces that they were serious and we realized that many things were still to come. After all, they say the best news is in the eye." Lere and Jay turned their eyes away from the new settlement simultaneously.

"We also believed them," he repeated. "To answer your question we could have asked them questions. We could have told them something they would never forget if they were telling us lies. But who understands people from Gaborone? As I said, fear gripped the whole place there. Their eyes and words held terror for us. We learnt later that others had been relocated too from other settlements inside the reserve. The end of our people's existence is near at hand and perhaps you could offer us a solution." He looked away and sniffed.

Jay said nothing and coughed.

Lere turned his head toward him. He looked at Jay who was facing south. And looking in the same direction, the old man saw his own wife emerging from her newly-made wood and branch thatched hut. She was attracted by the conversation between the two men.

For a moment, Jay felt that he had been betrayed, cheated by his family and people. Why did they accept the compensation? Even his wives! He vowed silently to denounce everything, his people, the authorities, the new settlement and compensation, its development and civilization.

Lere took away his eyes from a Kori bastard bird which flew in the air like the tiny aircraft he had seen many times in the reserve ferrying tourists. Would he see it again in the CKGR? Something like a spear surged up and down in his heart. He sighed loudly and looked away from Jay as if he wanted to hide the pain in his eyes. But something more than pain made him bow his head: it was shame. He had failed to protect the people and their ancestral home.

The world was moving fast and he was fearful. He waited for Jay to speak. Perhaps as part of this generation he would interpret the meaning of the relocation, of this strange event. But Jay did not, could not speak. He twisted his nose in disdain, open contempt. He held his head in his cupped hands and swallowed something that seemed to refuse to go down his throat.

"Perhaps I was too long at the hunting expedition," Jay said at last, almost speaking to himself. He thought of Ghanzi where he had stayed for some time. But the name just came and it choked his nostrils. As it had been, with the settlements inside it, the wild fruits, animals, the sand dunes, the herbs for any ailment, tourists from all over the world, wildlife officers patrolling.

"Where are the others," Lere's wife, Mawee broke into Jay's thoughts without any greeting. She did not show any indication that she would take a seat.

"I mean the people with whom you went hunting?"

It was then that Jay remembered that he had not told the others with whom he had gone hunting that he was tracking his family. He had forgotten to inform the hunting crew, which had visited him from settlements outside the reserve, that he had lost his family.

He looked away from Mawee to the east. Several new thatched huts lay sprawled in rows. Turning away to the west, Jay saw shining corrugated metal houses with solar panels, perhaps for government officials. There were also football and netball grounds.

"And you too, mother," Jay said accusingly focusing his stare on Mawee. He did not attempt to answer her question.

"Why did you and father agree to move from our home?" Jay made as if to rise to his feet. But he slumped back on the log. Mawee just shrugged her shoulders. Jay turned his eyes and swayed his legs in the direction of his own wife.

He was as annoyed as a male ostrich would be at a female one which left a game ranger unharmed after snatching its last eggs.

"Xhwaashe," he called his wife now ignoring his mother who was about to answer him. But his wife was quiet too. She wept. She did not understand. It was like his words instilled fear in her which muzzled her from answering. Or his words had no meaning. Xhwaashe remained frozen, the way Jay had found her. She rocked her small child on her back, a baby whose crying had risen since Jay's arrival. It was as if the baby had been missing its father.

0-0-0-0-0

Perhaps it missed the CKGR. By now a few elderly people had gathered. Jay wanted to ask everything, everyone what really had happened; he was growing increasingly annoyed with his family's silence.

Some people embraced him while others sobbed as if they could not believe he was still alive.

"My son, the British," Lere turned his eyes to Jay as if continuing an argument within his head, a thorn pricking his heart and forcing words to come out.

"They are the ones who gave us this place. I mean the reserve that we were relocated from, the CKGR. They are also the ones who protected this country and gave it independence. They are the ones who trained and educated the people who are ruling us today. They gave the power to the sons of this country in 1966. Those sons were trained there. Their ways, you can safely say, are the ways of the British. In other words their ways are different from us. They can reverse the decisions that were made by the British." The old man paused. With the silence he had created, he sighed and swallowed hard. His voice was shaking.

"As I was saying," the old man continued, rubbing away an insect that had crawled onto his shoulder. "You can see that the sons of this country have the power to reverse what the British did. Perhaps what most of you would like to know is why we were given this place."

He paused again to recover his breath.

"This place was created shortly before independence because the British wanted to take us away from the oppression of the European farmers in Ghanzi. Even now, if you go there you will find our people, the Basarwa children, being oppressed in the farms and ranches in Ghanzi as is the case everywhere in this country. But there is nothing that we can do. We, the Basarwa have no modern education. We know nothing about modernity, about civilization because we have never liked it before. We have nothing. They say we are nobody. So if you ask me, there is nothing we can do. We cannot refuse when we are told by people who have everything and make laws; laws we cannot understand."

There were traces of pain in his words which seemed to echo in the far north, reaching the sacred Aha and Tsodilo hills. These were the holy places where the Basarwa ancestors dwelt.

Lere placed his chin in his cupped hand. He shifted one leg onto the other and looked at his son, Jay.

"Father, you are telling us old stories." Jay shook his head bitterly, unable to pick an object on which to focus his concentration about what happened in the past. "You are right. That is background information to help us understand how we came to be in this position, But let me remind some of you that this is not the time for old stories. If we had not been lied to, that so-and-so used to be our masters, we would not be in this position. This reserve, in fact the whole of the Southern African region, belongs to our people. We are as old as this land. Why do you think we are called the Real People...?"

"I think I must say something before you go any further." It was Qoero interrupting him. She was an old woman who spoke with a soft voice. Her skin had sagged so much that it looked like a football goal net. Her eyes were sunken and as she spoke it seemed they would disappear at any time.

"I agree with Lere," she said. "It could be true that we were moved to this place because of the European farmers' oppression. Ever since then we have lived happily here. Strange things never touched us. The whole desert is our home. We the Basarwa, own this desert. The story I got from my father who died during the time of the great locust swarm when people like Jay were born, is that we were always pushed by stronger groups. First it was the Boers from Sausa Aforika (corruption of South Africa). We landed at the then Kgalagadi, what is now called Kalahari Desert. The word Kgalagadi means thirst and struggle for survival. That explains the harsh conditions we had to endure; climatic conditions and the wounds inflicted upon us by our so-called masters even today. Don't we carry the scars even today? she asked and then continued.

"We have tattooed tears. You will never find a happy face borne by even one of our people. It is not that we were wanderers; those who were stronger than us, those who love war, forced us. As a peace loving people we had no choice but to find sanctuary in this desert. And now the relocation."

The old woman, wept as if she had been told about the death of a dear relative. Perhaps the CKGR, their ancestral home, was on the verge of death. Qoero buried her head in her hands, to hide them from the eyes of children and other people who were listening. When she raised her head, her eyes were moist, like the desert's morning fog.

"We can lay claim to the whole country." She gestured at Jay. "And other countries in the south, Jay is right." Qoero tried to control her aging, trembling voice. Jay nodded and looked away.

"We will not be considered the lowest of all the people,"

Jay said. "We will not be the cheapest people, held in contempt if all along we had not agreed to be pushed and agreed to leave our ancestors' graves behind. We were stripped of our dignity. Let's go back to our homesteads at once."

The meeting was divided. Some agreed that they should go back to the reserve while others said they could not.

"The world was ruined many years ago," Lere continued, pleading with his son and those who supported him to come away from the danger that he foresaw as an old man who had seen better times. "I saw the sun before you, and I can see that the world is coming to an end."

Jay pulled dark smoke from his cigarette and shook his head.

"If I had my way," He made as if to rise, but only succeeded in slumping back onto the log once again. "I would have stopped my wives from coming here. The people who relocated them would rather have killed me. But it is not too late. We cannot be stripped of our dignity like that. We are going back home."

Jay held up his head. Thorn trees like the Mosu and Moselesele spread out endlessly around the new settlement. It was called New Xade. It was dry, sandy and cracked soil spread and drained quickly as it was reduced to dust by wildlife and police trucks. There were also sand dunes and some deciduous trees.

Jay talked of Molapo, of Kekangwe, of Metsimanong, of Gugama and Kikao. All these were settlements in the CKGR.

"These places are our homes," Jay said. "We inherited them from our ancestors. We are also from the Baxanako clan." Jay had a way with words. His eyes shrank a little like a child about to cry. Blinking with every word, a mischievous smile spread slowly on his face.

Lere looked at him. "But it seems you are in such a hurry that you do not even want to consider the danger that lies ahead. Even if you want to go home now, remember that the hurried arrow kills little game." With these words, Lere wore a sullen face.

But for Jay as he stood up to go home, home being CKGR, another thought lingered on his mind. He turned toward his youngest wife who was sitting behind him.

"Motse," he said, raising his voice unnecessarily as she was only an arms-length away. "What did I tell you about going against the voices of the gods?"

He wiped away perspiration from his eyebrows. Motse stretched her bent legs in front of her. She raised her eyes and looked at the senior wife for words. But Xhwaashe looked away, disowning her.

"Has this development and civilization gone into your head?" he asked. Now she had to answer, for a volcano was about to explode. Jay's eyes were red with accumulated fury which had been directed at those who had relocated his wives, his people. Now the anger was focussed on the helpless young woman, his wife.

"No," she said weeping like a child. "They haven't. We were told not to go back."

Jay rose to his feet, ignoring the explanation. "Who told you?"

The reluctance to answer by his wife, mixed with silent cries of his people now distilled into an urgency to act; to go back home, without his family.

0-0-0-0-0

Now, Jamana turning on the ignition awaked Jay from this long reverie. "You dozed off as soon as I went to see the lawyers," he said. He glanced at Jay with the look that sought to defy him.

"I was day dreaming about what happened on the day that I found that my family had been stolen. So what is the next step?" asked Jay.

"Revolution," said Jamana turning his head slowly to ensure that the lane of the road to Gaborone from Lobatse town centre was safe before he could join it. Jay thought he had heard the word before but could not place it.

"But not today," Jay said. "I think tomorrow, we can start the revolution. They will know what we are capable of." Jamana did not answer. He was negotiating the curves of the road and the potholes. There was silence. Eventually Jay dozed off.

# Chapter Five

Jay and his companions including his everyday associate, Jamana, set out the following day. This was after their arrival in New Xade from Lobatse High Court.

Each man carried a bow and more than one arrow. As the sun rose, they left the new settlement behind them. The revolution had begun.

"You know," Jay said. "A chief who takes away his people's property is like a knife that cuts the poor man's luxury. How can we lose our homes to men who already have enough resources? Why? How? We have to go back home."

"I think it is because of the many lies told about us," said one of the men. "In fact lies written about us and now we have been stripped of our dignity."

"True," agreed Jamana. "It was once said that we have no words of our own, that we did not know how to make babies."

Jay nodded several times. "Nothing could be more misleading. You know when a Mosarwa speaks, it is an omen." He looked vaguely at the sun. Their shadows were now staring at them, beneath their feet.

Another man chuckled and nodded. "Jay you are giving us a voice. Never before has there been someone like you from our people. I heard that people are surprised that you are one of us."

"But such words could only have been said during the days of our forefathers. Not when I'm alive. We are going back home. You know before going to hunt on the day my family was relocated, my body communicated it to me. I had a throbbing on my feet."

"True" said Jamana. "It was a warning, a sign that you were going to take a long journey. They say a story is like wind. It comes from a far off quarter and we feel it."

"And my body never lies to me, Jamana," said Jay. "Just like the way it talked to me the day your grandfather died. Remember I told you I had a throbbing on top of my eyebrow. Something ominous was coming and I saw it; your grandfather passed away."

There was silence.

"That is even so," the two men said simultaneously,

"The sun never sets without fresh news," agreed Jay, looking behind at the other men who followed him closely. "But to accept relocation after what I have learnt about the effects of development brought about by those who are civilized in other parts of the world and places I have been to in this country, means that I would have agreed to let my people die. People have to know that I'm like the adhesive grass. I will stick fast to fighting against relocation. I did not have to ask myself, whether this was a good or bad thing for my people."

"What we have to find out from the authorities," another man said, "is how the reserve was created. Why are they interested in our desert, our only heritage, after so many years? What have they discovered there?"

"There is no need to ask such questions," Jay interrupted now smelling the words of betrayal, like the words of his father, Lere, who seemed to support the relocation. His eyes narrowed and constricted.

"That land is our undisputed home," he said. "If you ask me, I have no time for such kind of questions. How can you ask a man who knows the truth such questions, when you want to go home after wandering aimlessly around the world and after you were abducted from your home?"

The sun was approaching what the people of Kalahari

Desert call the 'ground level' when Jay and his companion reached their destination.

There was a big board with white lettering near the gate showing the name of the place, the reserve: CKGR. Underneath the name of the place were names of settlements inside the reserve: Molapo, Gugama, Mothomelo, Kikao.

Again, on a thatched shade that hovered over the main gate, like a blackboard in a classroom, were words scribbled skilfully with thatch: XADE.

A barbed wire fence ran around the reserve. Tourists went to and fro. There was an office where tourists registered near the gate. They parked their cars and trucks outside near the fence. Some of the tourists travelled in vans, others in trucks driven by tourist guides. A junior officer went inside the office after Jay and his companion had told him about their mission.

Back from the office, the junior officer led another wildlife officer to Jay and his companions. The other man was of a spare frame. He was evidently the senior officer as he had many pins on his shoulders, denoting his lofty position. He was at a loss to see more than ten men with bows and arrows slung across their shoulders.

He greeted them generally in the customary manner, directing his words at everyone.

All the men returned his greetings except Jay, who remained silent.

"My name is Dikai Sennye. What is it that you want?"

He surveyed the men with his bored eyes behind rimmed glasses. There was silence. Jay was seized by an irresistible thought that left him shivering, gasping for action. He thought of going back to the new settlements and returning with all his people back into the reserve.

Why go home alone? Where were the children and their mothers? And to think that the meat he had left inside the reserve a few weeks earlier before he followed them was rotting in the scorching sun! But the thought of the meat, the desire to mend the boreholes for water killed the desire to go back and call his people from the new settlements, New Xade and Kaudwane. The urge to peep at the meat and the ruins made by the authorities brought hunger and thirst. He missed CKGR more than ever. Perhaps more than he had missed his wives when he found that they had been relocated. He had to act now.

"Are you tourists?" Sennye asked impatiently bursting into Jay's thoughts. His tone carried a mixture of uncertainty, doubt and mockery. To Jay, this was an insult or it sounded like one. The cobra's muscles around Jay's neck expanded like a tyre being inflated. The cobra was ready to strike. The eyes blinked rapidly like a robot with a fault. He was sending a message to Sennye. But the senior wild officer, with the powers bestowed upon him by his superiors, looked away ignoring Jay's threats. Perhaps just like his superiors had done when Jay went around the world telling the international community to help his people go back home. Who would listen to a 'thing' like him? Who was he anyway? But Jay's lips parted. His eyes widened slightly as if in fear.

Jay fished into his pocket.

"Not an identity card," Sennye laughed such that his protruding teeth were left glistening in the sun. He raised an eyebrow and shrugged his shoulders. "I'm sorry, I cannot let you in."

Jay's eyes narrowed in time to his flaring nose.

"How can you let people go inside our home and yet refuse to allows in?" he asked. He was referring to a French tourist who had just signed at the gate and was allowed to go in.

Sennye raised an eyebrow again and answered a phone

call from a small device, which to Jay looked like a small radio. His eyes were still fixed on Jay. He pointed at Jay and then to Jay's companions after he had finished talking on the radio. Sennye nodded and coughed.

"Let me warn you that you are under rebellion watch."

Jay shrugged and inclined his head to one side.

"Whatever you say, we have to go home."

Although Sennye had been in the CKGR as a wildlife officer for more than a decade, never before had he seen a man with such courage. He might have seen Jay but he never knew or never thought that he could make such demands: Going Back To CKGR after the relocation of his people. Jay's voice had no trace of fear, not even apprehension, Sennye observed. And Jay was resolute as though he had control over the whole country. Or as if the Chief Justice had just sworn him in. Perhaps this was a new leader. What made him so bold?

"Don't you want to know what really happened?" Jay asked. But Sennye dismissed him with the shake of his hand and walked away.

"Wait there," Jay said following Sennye. "Do you know or don't you that the place you have been patrolling all along is my home? You and other wildlife officers are my bodyguards." Sennye strained his ears refusing to believe the evidence of his ears. He let out a shuddering sigh.

"What? No!"

"But if you do not," Jay said loudly for effect. "This is my home, you have been providing me, my people and our wild animals with security. You are our guards and herd boys as well." Sennye shook his head. He was more shocked than offended. He bit his lower lips.

"Has this place been your home or is there something inside now that makes you think it's your home? Or have you been given powers that now you can..."

"Lately we have... In fact we do not see any reason why we should remind anyone that this is our home. Even a blind man never loses his way to his home. After all, the tongue of a newly born baby never loses its way to the breast."

"Perhaps there is something we do not know apart from the fact that people were relocated," said Sennye in a calm voice.

"Indeed you don't," Jay nodded his head. "You are just a servant. After all, you were born yesterday," though Sennye looked like a man in his late sixties or older than Jay. He shrugged his shoulders as if he also did not know his age.

"What is it that you want exactly? Perhaps we can help."

"For now, I would say there is nothing except that I want to go home," Jay said.

"Haven't you heard the news? It is all over the newspapers, I'm told. When returning from hunting, I found that my family, my people have been stolen and loaded in big trucks. Don't you know that they were stolen? I'm looking for the stolen people of the Kalahari. I tried to find them at the court and didn't find them. I think they are in the reserve!"

In response, Sennye shook his head and sighed again.

Jay looked at the junior wildlife officer and then at Sennye. "The whole thing seemed unreal at first." Jay said this the way a lost man would explain how he failed to find his way back home. "If it had not happened to me, I would not have believed it myself. I found that my people had been stolen, their huts destroyed; captured, you may say. Indeed as one of my companions put it, it happened the way Shaka, king of the Zulu captured people during a war with a minor tribe. Do I need to tell you that I ran from one settlement to another? There were no huts, no people."

Jay paused and rubbed his eyebrows. He turned towards his companions.

"I tried to take some of my people back this morning

from where they have been hidden from their ancestors, but they are still shocked. They have not yet recovered from the trauma and I couldn't help them."

Jay paused again. He spoke slowly as if he wanted his listeners to understand each word.

"In fact I tried to wake my people up from the sleep of so many years but the police arrested me saying I was disturbing the peace in a peaceful and democratic country. I did not know that waking up ones' own people or removing scales from their eyes was an offence. I have just been released from prison as we speak. And I'm going home right now to look for my stolen people."

"Your stolen people?"

"Yes."

"But there are no huts anymore," said Sennye almost losing his patience. It seemed the little respect he had had for Jay was vanishing, disappearing. He measured Jay as if he now understood who he was, from his story. That after all Jay was not a tourist but a man who someone from a major tribe like Sennye could not look at twice. He was a 'thing.'

"I'm going there to build the huts so that when I succeed in waking up my people they would find huts already built."

"But I do not understand," Sennye said doubting Jay's sanity now. "Did you beat up some of your people while forcing them to come over here?"

"'No," Jay said without flinching. "It is the other way round. I was beaten up by the security agents and my people were forced to stay there in the new settlements."

"Is that all?"

"Yes and No," Jay said. "Because it is a long story and we might spend many years talking about it and perhaps die here before I return home."

"Oh I see," said Sennye with a note of finality.

"Let me tell you something before I'm arrested," Jay said. "I told the police that I had left my people alone when I went for a hunting trip." He wet his lips and shielded his face from the rising sun. "Otherwise they would not have been stolen. In a way, I was responsible, I could have protected them. That is all for now."

Sennye nodded several times as if he was beginning to believe and understand Jay's story.

When Jay continued speaking, it was as if he was not including his companions. "But can you let me go home?"

In response Sennye only sighed very hard.

"We want to go home." Jay repeated. He made as if he would rush to the gate. But he only took a step and stopped.

"Home?" Sennye looked at his junior for further explanation, stunned. It was as if it was the first time he had heard Jay mentioning the word 'home'.

Jay looked at his companions for support. "Yes, home."

The two wildlife officials laughed. Still trying to shake off the giggles, Sennye raised his eyes towards Jay.

"We do not know of any homestead inside the reserve or stolen people." His junior nodded. Sennye raised an eyebrow and his large eyes were bulging like a man caught in the act of stealing.

"Perhaps you have already forgotten so soon that the people who were staying inside have been relocated. After all, in my whole life I have never heard of a home in a reserve where wild animals are protected."

At these words, Jay's face registered furrows, compelling his listeners to turn away their eyes and not look at him. His eyes were immobile. He breathed hard. He tried to control a burning sensation in his nostrils. He sniffed in rapid succession. And at that point in his anger, he blinked twice or so.

"I think I must warn you that I'm Jay from the Kalahari Desert." He shook his hand and pointed at the two wildlife officials to emphasize his warning.

Sennye looked away from Jay to the gate.

"Indeed from the Kalahari Desert." His hands were on his waist. There was no mockery in Sennye's voice now. One has to be careful with a strange fellow like this one, he reflected.

"At least you know that this place is a reserve. If that is why you came here I think I must go at once and make permits for licensed hunters and register tourists. As you can see they are coming in large numbers. From the UK, USA, France, Russia."

"I said we want to go home." Jay pointed at the sparsely populated trees far in the north, indicating that his mission was urgent.

He now moved toward the gate almost following Sennye. He stopped outside.

Sennye went inside the office. Another tourist from Belgium came in. He went inside the office, filled forms and paid park fees. He then signed on the register, got behind the wheel of a rented truck and drove off.

Dark clouds moved towards the south. There was no time to lose, Jay reflected silently eyeing the pregnant clouds. But before he could do anything, thunder rumbled. Suddenly it rained heavily. The raindrops blinded Jay and soaked him and his compatriots. The sudden downpour formed small pools in the Savannah grassland.

Jay was about to wipe the rain away from his face but his hand froze in mid-air. A truck full of tourists arrived. His mind having been seized with the loss of his people, Jay unexpectedly bolted for the gate at the same time as the truck. The driver braked, jerking the truck forward before coming to a halt.

The screaming and frightened passengers, who were nearly hurled out, rushed out.

A few of them had wet themselves in shock; others buried their heads in their hands, calling for their parents to come to their aid.

The junior officer was the first to see the accident. As the flash storm ended, he had been struggling with Jay's men who were forcing their way into the reserve.

The senior officer called his junior to attend to the tourists and the accident. His angry voice reached his junior at once. However, the junior officer tried to explain that he was struggling with the other men, but the screaming tourists drowned his voice. He left the men and went to help the senior officer. At the senior wildlife official's request, the driver grabbed Jay. But Jay put up strong resistance although it became clear that the driver was stronger than him, as he was unable to break away from the grip of a single hand. Still in the driver's vice, Jay's hand wriggled mechanically and manoeuvred like a worm towards the man's zip, which he undid. The driver immediately shouted like a billy goat being castrated, begging Jay to leave his manhood alone or at least grab any other part of his body. But before Jay could teach him a lesson, five wildlife officials gathered at the scene.

They took Jay behind the office by the gate. As the driver of the truck smarted from the ordeal, he realized that Jay must have lost or wanted something big inside the reserve. And to him, Jay was a good fighter. Unexpectedly, a burning desire, which he could not understand, seized him. He wanted to see Jay, the man who had wrestled him on thorn bushes. Just as he arrived behind the office, the wildlife officers had overpowered Jay and he fell, first with his face and his body followed with a thud. The driver tried to turn Jay's face.

"He is okay," said one of the officers. "Don't worry he will be fine." The driver ignored the assurances. He had been in
42

the CKGR for a long time; in fact he was born in the CKGR. Perhaps he knew or had met him during one of his trips in Ghanzi.

"My ancestors!" The driver buried his head in his hands after turning Jay's face.

Jay's face only stared at the driver. His eyelids bulged like a freshly slaughtered goat. The driver rushed to the truck, past the still shocked tourists. Thinking that he must be taking a gun from the truck, two wildlife officers rushed after him. The driver jumped into the truck, made a dramatic U-turn and swayed the vehicle at high speed. It smashed the gate and its impact echoed in the Kalahari sand dunes like thunder. The truck's engine switched off. The driver's face smashed the windscreen and blood oozed from his faces perhaps maybe bloodier than Jay's face was.

No one understood what had happened. Everything had happened so fast. When the prison officers went back, they found Jay the way they had left him when they attended to the driver. He was lying on his back, sprawled like a fully-grown python. When he saw them, Jay made some efforts to raise his head but only achieved little success. He groaned and moaned like the engine of an old train. He tried to mutter something. The officers rushed and tried to get what he had said, as his life slipped away. But Jay's mouth and eyes closed. He gripped the sand dunes with both hands, the way he would have done during the sacred trance dance.

# Chapter Six

Judges leaving their comfortable courts in search of justice in the desert! Something considered a God-forsaken place, just like its inhabitants. But CKGR's hidden treasure was a terrible truth and the best-kept if not forgotten secret.

The relocation itself had the country in the grips of suspense like a half-dead man hanging from a tree. Many people had left their professional lives to peep into CKGR. It was a desire, an irresistible longing that was perhaps like the fruit that was said to have been eaten by Adam in the Bible after he was advised to do so by his wife, Eve.

People did not understand - no one did - that a man only armed with eland horns attached to beads around his head could stand up in public and denounce relocation from a desert, a place with the harshest conditions. It was the newspaper people, politicians, lawyers, judges, priests, businessmen, bank professionals, professors and human rights organizations who discovered him. But how he was created was a mystery. Everyone held his or her breath. Analysts said the country was only a step away from destruction. The revolution of people who were considered less than human-things was near at hand. Everyone across the globe waited to be entertained. But the three judges, being learned men and woman, knew that justice delayed is justice denied!

And even up to the day, it had at first seemed unreal, untrue, that the judges were there. The three judges! For the sake of justice! But still it sounded false, unreal.

It could not be true. A High Court Judge in the desert?

Now Jay shook his head. "Molefe, did you say the judges were here?"

Molefe nodded. "Yes. They were all over CKGR before coming here to New Xade."

Now Jay shook his head again. A sly smile spread on his face.

"Jamana can you believe this?" he asked. "Anyway, I told you that the sun never sets without fresh news." In response Jamana smiled revealing protruding teeth.

He wet his thin lips with saliva.

"You have attracted attention like Marietta Bosch," said Jamana, referring to the South African white woman hung in Botswana on conviction of killing her lover's wife.

Jay sighed and laughed slightly. "But I haven't killed anyone. Molefe are you sure they were judges? Have I killed the country by telling the truth?"

Molefe was silent for a moment and then nodded again, taking his eyes away from a notebook on which he was writing something. "Yes they were." He paused. "As Jamana always says, a story is like wind; it comes from a far off quarter, and we feel it. If I had not met them myself I wouldn't have believed the story."

Jay's curiosity grew. He sighed very hard.

"What were they looking for?"

Now it was Molefe's turn to wear the sly smile. "They were looking for you and the CKGR. They said, Jay Setlhare. In fact the case is going to be heard in New Xade and it has now attracted the whole world the way sugar attracts a swarm of bees. I heard that they were waiting for you to be discharged from hospital. Is it true that the driver who assisted in arresting you at the CKGR gate is your younger brother?"

Jay's eyes narrowed. He waved his hand in the air as if celebrating having achieved his mission. "Indeed this is not a small matter. Are they saying I was discharged from hospital? I'm from prison, and I can't remember how many times I have been in those prisons. Regarding my brother arresting me and joining the enemies who have stolen our people, I can't blame him. There was a time when we could talk about that Molefe, sitting around the fire roasting eland meat and dancing to the gods to give us more days to live. But there is no chance to do that anymore. No my friend, tell me another story before I'm arrested for trying to go back to the CKGR. I'm readying myself for another battle at the CKGR gate. I know they will bring guns and their obese stomachs full of all the country's resources accumulated in their bellies. We will confront them with our arrows, thirsty as we will be like orphans."

Jamana nodded several times, glancing at Jay and Molefe as he did so.

Molefe laughed nervously and picked up a cup full of water. "Do you want me to talk about the application we, the First People of Kalahari, have launched at the Lobatse High Court? What I can say is that the Court has moved from Lobatse to this part of the country. It was said that people all over the world would like to see us giving evidence while taking instructions from our ancestors as you had said. It was said that this would be the wonder to beat all wonders. Newspaper people from all over the world were here as well. There was no movement for tourists this morning."

Jay grinned slightly and shook his head.

"Did they say anything about letting us go back home?"

He lit a cigarette and sucked at it, eyeing Molefe. But the other man simply shook his head unable to speak because of the water he was still swallowing.

"I'm ready for whatever," Jay said. "After all the fire log burns him who stirs it up. I have started the fight and will fight to the bitter end come what may. I would like to recover my stolen people."

Molefe looked away and put the cup down. He watched the smoke as it curled before he spoke up.

"They were only taking down and studying huts and everything in the CKGR that we used to own. They didn't say anything about stolen people."

Jay's grin turned into something like a snarl. There was a growl that sounded like thunder in his throat.

"Can you hear what he is saying?" It was as if Jay was asking the ancestors to be his witnesses.

Molefe sighed sensing accusation in Jay's words and in his immobile eyes.

"What should I have done?" It was not a question but a statement. "I didn't start the relocation, Jay. Neither did I reveal the secret treasures hidden in this desert to diamond explores."

Jay's lips were trembling. His trips across the globe seemed to have created a new dignity, a new human being had been born, a man perhaps different from anyone he had heard of or seen in the country, Molefe observed.

"Instead of celebrating the arrival of the court in CKGR you should have told the judges to tell their educated friends not to steal our land. They must also start learning to respect the Real People: the first inhabitants of all the land in the whole world. Why did they steal our people? That is the question, you should have asked them instead of putting your hands between your laps like a woman whose child has caught her naked with another man."

Molefe turned his eyes to Jamana in appeal, for support. But the other man lowered his eyes as if he did not want to reveal the secret kept in the desert, which even the missionary, Dr. David Livingstone, who discovered Victoria Falls in Zimbabwe had failed to detect.

Jay seemed to read Jamana's thoughts.

"Did they say anything about revealing the country's best kept secret to the world or helping us go back home?" Instead of answering Jay, Molefe asked a question.

He showed no sign that he had heard Jay's question. "You did not tell me how Survival International would assist us.    Did they say they would help us go back home?"

Jay was silent. Molefe's question had transported him to his meeting with the leader of the British human rights organization, Survival International in London, in the company of Jamana.

0-0-0-0-0

"Even if it means killing my mother," Jay had told the leader of Survival International, Steven Garry. "I will never give up when it comes to the CKGR; even if politicians were to ask me to sell my three wives at an auction sale. Is it not the modern way of getting promotion for a top post in the country these days? But I couldn't. I wouldn't." At that moment a young woman had appeared. Garry and Jamana had turned their eyes toward her with Jay following suit. The young woman had on a blue top and tight light yellow trouser. Jay had to narrow his eyes to convince himself that she was not naked. Her breasts were so firm that had it not been for the love Jay had for the CKGR, perhaps he would have forgotten why he was in London. Her face was so smooth that beauty therapists would have recommended her for Miss World Beauty Pageant had it not been her height. She was short.

"Meet Mr. Jay Setlhare and Jamana Obonye from CKGR in the Kalahari Desert," Garry had said to the young woman after she had closed the door behind her, gently like a nurse tending the wounds of a badly burnt patient.

"Gentlemen, this is Rose, she is the Secretary of Survival International." A captivating smile beamed across Rose's face as she nodded. It was Jamana and Garry who were doing most of the talking, Rose noted, and she did not understand why. But she suddenly did when Jamana looked in Jay's direction and spoke in a language full of clicks. Rose thought she would cut her tongue were she to imitate him. To her, the click sounds were like the clucking of hens, but she instantly hated herself for thinking ill of the visitors, their lost friends.

Garry turned to Rose who was still slightly amused by the language spoken by the two visitors.

"Have you been to CKGR? What do you know about it?"

Rose shook her head and extended her hand to shake Jay's. The Secretary observed that the other man's hand was firm like a vice-grip. When it came to Jamana, he greeted her in such fluent English that she temporarily forgot that he had been speaking a language full of clicks.

Rose grinned and nodded her head several times. "I think I have been there through reading tourism magazines and a book that was written by a certain South African author who happens to be a good friend of our Prince here in Britain."

A smile that could have indicated joy or mockery flickered on Garry's eyes. "That is true. There is something that people cannot resist about the CKGR including our own British Prince and the authorities of that country itself."

"Ok," Rose said with warmth as if she grew interested in knowing the Kalahari Desert's secret. Garry's hairy eyebrows narrowed. "It's like everyone from every corner of the globe wants to go and testify at the great case that involves Jay's people and their government."

Garry knew that Survival International's reputation would suffer should the case before the Lobatse High Court fail to resume. While in the CKGR, Garry had stared into the wilderness thinking how he could assist Jay and his people. He had listened to the continuous buzz of crickets mingling with planes, and knew that he too loved the place as much as Jay did. The Kalahari sun had turned his skin into pale leather. He had also thought Jay's words would make the United Nations react. His hairy skin concealed in a black safari suit, his eyes were like a frozen lake. Jay did not look like a Mosarwa, Garry had observed when they first met in the CKGR. He looked more like a Red Indian. Not short, as historians had described the Basarwa in African history books. Garry was to laugh later when Jay told him that he was born a few months after the war of Hitler, or during the time which the people of the CKGR called "the time of great locusts."

0-0-0-0-0

Jay was jolted out of his daydream by Molefe who sighed as though he had something strange to tell them, some abomination. Something that Jay had not expected nor understood seemed to leave his body when his eyes met Molefe's. He felt drained, weak at the knees as if his bone marrow was being sucked out. On the other hand, Jay's glazed eyes also imparted little hope in Molefe.

"Perhaps if we get help from local organizations the authorities would let us go back to the CKGR rather than seeking help from international organizations," said

Molefe with words that sought to distance themselves from any conspiracy between him and the authorities during Jay and Jamana's sojourn to Europe. Jay plucked out another cigarette and fished in his pockets for matches. He took out a stick and struck the side of the box, lighting his cigarette. Molefe had expected frustration, but it was a smile of content that now danced on Jay's face. "Survival says they are going to launch a dangerous campaign that will shock the authorities; a campaign which the world has never seen."

Molefe looked into the distance, searching the dark wilderness like a police searchlight. His mind having found nothing, returned to the issue at hand. "But remember that we have made promises to Ditshwanelo, Kuru Development Trust, churches and the authorities themselves that we would hold negotiations as to how we can return to the CKGR."

Jay shrugged his shoulders. Should he reveal what plans he had with Survival International? No. He should not take chances with a character like Molefe, though he was the FPK's secretary. Anyone could be bribed into selling the ancestral land, the CKGR, and its hidden wonders that had caused his people to disappear from it.

"Do we have a choice now?" Jay's voice was threatening to burst the cobra arteries around his neck. "Tell me Molefe, do we?"

There was silence. Then Molefe spoke up. "Yes we do."

"Which is?"

"Negotiations."

"No, we can't."

"Why?"

"Because we don't trust anyone," Jay said almost rising to his feet. "In addition, we have lost our people because they are said to be more worthless than the soil they have been staying on since time immemorial. No one will help us find them in this country, you know that. Remember that a man tracing his father's eland does not give up just because he cannot find its traces on the dry sand."

"But what about Survival International?"

"We trust them, Molefe."

"Jay, don't behave as if you are the only one with sense. People will say you sold their country to the people across the sea."

Indeed The Three Chiefs who went to Britain in 1885 to seek protection against the South African Boers' invasion and the destructive diamond explorer, Cecil John

Rhodes's dream of Cape to Cairo road, must have had little impression on Jay. For it seemed he was looking for another protectorate.

Jay's eyebrows were raised slightly as he slumped back on the wooden stool. "Molefe, listen to me." His eyes were shining. "As you said earlier on, it is not Jay who brought about this relocation issue. I'm not the one who made people develop interest in a desert, our home, to look for precious resources that made Europe what it is today. And I cannot fold my arms and let people here and their international friends come over here and fatten their pockets with the CKGR's treasures. We have no choice. In fact we never had choice. We will wait for assistance from Survival International." He wiped something across his face, which Molefe could not discern due to the fading light.

All the time, Jamana sat with his legs crossed and his head in his hands. He seemed trapped between the sweet sadness of melodies from the birds and bitter exchanges between the two men. The words and the sad melodies seemed to deepen the destiny of the CKGR's residents and their case at the High Court. The images of the people came to merge with his own and those of the two men and he thought he saw them crushed under the sand dunes. He could not take his eyes away from the terrified eyes of the CKGR residents. There was a note of sadness in the two men's conversation. Jamana now spread his legs before him as his grandmother used to do when sorting out wild fruits. He ran his hand over his freshly shaved head, as Jay and Molefe turned their eyes towards him.

"We have spent a lot of time running away from slavery," Jamana yawned as if awakening from a long dream. "If the judges find us guilty of breaking the law by refusing to relocate from the CKGR, so be it."

Jay nodded and his eyes blinked quickly like an orphan whose toy has been snatched away by a cruel caretaker. He let out a loud sigh as if Jamana had read him section 203 of the Constitution that dealt with the death penalty.

"Whatever it was that led to the protectorate in 1885, the fruits have not been tasted in these parts of the country. People say we are sell outs. Sell outs where?

We have never sent our children to European schools. We will keep on speaking with contempt to those who say we were not forced out of our homes in the CKGR.

We want justice, nothing else. Let the judges bring us justice though we are not sure if their employer would allow them to. After that we will get the truth as to why our people were stolen."

The tension on Jay's face that emerged when Jamana talked about being found guilty by the court slowly turned into relief. Jay smiled weakly but a flicker in his eyes.

"We need someone we can trust in this struggle and we are waiting impatiently for Survival International. They have already found a lawyer for us to help tear the veil that hides the truth about the CKGR, you know that."

With these words, Jay pulled Jamana by the hand, leaving Molefe, with the notebook still on his lap in the FPK office in Ghanzi. The longing to be in the CKGR and find his people was like a cigarette addiction. He had to get advice from the ancestors and tell the judges the ancestors' instructions even if it meant boycotting Survival International and their lawyer, Benny.

# Chapter Seven

The CKGR is the size of Belgium. It is the home of various species of wild animals and the residents were, or are, hunters and gathers. No one seemed to have bothered about what exactly lay in that place, not even the great Southern African explorers like Robert Moffat and Dr David Livingstone. But now everyone was scrambling for it. It had become a source of interest to mineral explorers and tourism big shots, who wanted to unveil or benefit from the hidden treasure that the Basarwa were sitting on or merely failed to utilize. In the summer, the place looked desolate, but during spring, it was a sight to behold, with clusters of Acacia and Savannah bush veldt. There was also great swathes of unending grassland, so appealing to the eye that it seemed to have been cut by a skilled lawn mower.

Indeed the CKGR was a haven of wild animals. To the Basarwa lawyer, Garden Benny from New Square Chambers in London, the CKGR reminded him of the Garden of Eden he had read about in the Bible's Genesis. He observed that it was bigger than some countries that he had been to. There were pans, sand dunes, Savannah bush veldt and beds of dry grass especially during summer.

As they stood in the open in New Xade, Benny noted that Jay's eyes always looked equal to any challenge when he spoke about the CKGR. Jay had the eyes of a cobra and like a cobra he was always ready to strike.

On the other hand, there was this quality, a kindness that Jay also observed in the British lawyer. In the presence of Benny, nothing reminded Jay that he was a lesser human being. Benny would listen earnestly and interrupt only when necessary. Perhaps Jay and his people were human beings lacking rights. "It's a strange case on its own."

Dumelang Phoko, the local instructing attorney agreed with Benny. He said this with a relaxed smile. Suddenly the smile changed into a severe expression when he added, "But we cannot fold our arms. After all, that is what we have been trained to do. The story is simple: To go or not to go to the CKGR? That is the question." Being a former Harvard University student, Phoko was well acquainted with Shakespeare. His arguments in court were nothing more than poetry, always blended with eloquent English words. These touched the hearts of the audience, his clients, magistrates and judges the way a pastor would mesmerise his congregation into a trance. Perhaps that was the kind of English Queen Victoria would have been proud of, proof that indeed the slogan, 'Britain where the sun never sets was not out of place.'

Phoko chuckled now. But the smile on his face changed into something like a frown. He looked at Benny and then at Jay.

"We will file a new application," said Benny without taking his eyes off Jay. "This means we are going to start everything afresh." His voice reflected his smile, Jay observed and nodded.

The lawyer raised his eyebrow and nodded again as he glanced at Phoko.

"This is an important case not only in Africa." Turning his eyes from Phoko to Jay he said, "the world wants to know the truth. So you have to tell me why you don't want your people to be relocated from the CKGR. This means that you have to tell me nothing but the real truth."

Benny always referred to the Basarwa as Jay's people. It was as if to call them by their ethnic names, such as Bushmen or Basarwa as they were called in Botswana, was an offence that could hurt them.

A serene smile danced across Benny's face.

"I'm under the impression," Jay raised his eyebrows, "that Survival International has told you everything there is to know including the truth, hurtful as it may sound."

"They didn't tell me much," said Benny. "Except that you want to protect your way of life and ..."

"But can you really help us go back home and find my people?" Jay asked in a heartbroken voice. He shielded his yes from the rising sun, the smoke from his cigarette curling away lazily.

Benny clutched court files bigger than the ones Jay had seen from the state lawyer Peolwane and some South African lawyers who had represented him and his people when the case started at the Lobatse High Court. Even his robes were heavier than those of the other lawyers. It seemed the future, the life of the CKGR and his missing people were in those papers. Benny handled the papers with care as if he did not want to hurt the CKGR and its people as they stood there waiting for the court session to start. After all, Benny was from the Queen's land whose leader

Batswana fondly called Mma Mosadinyana, the lovely queen. Jay would later understand better what a document called the Constitution was, the mother of all laws in the country.

The British lawyer ran his hand over his bony head. Jay observed that the lawyer spoke through the nose, a nasal tone like most Britons he had heard as tourists in the CKGR. He spoke slowly as if everyone he spoke to was hard of hearing. He seldom let his stern face show and like many experienced advocates or attorneys, his head was bald. The case had reminded Benny, he told Jay, Phoko and Jamana now, of his days when he was a student doing a thesis on the lives of the Aborigine people in Australia. It had also reminded him of his days when he had represented certain tribes in Kenya and Tanzania. They were said to be minority groups with an ancient culture just like his present clients: Jay and his people.

"This is a human rights issue," he said turning to Jamana. "But it also has some political elements in it." Jay's eyes narrowed and blinked in rapid succession. Benny nodded.

"First I will have to find out why the reserve was created," said Benny. "I will also have to find out what exactly the real reasons for the relocation are."

Jay nodded and chuckled unexpectedly as if he had just discovered the truth about the reasons for the relocation.

"But can you really help us go home, find my people or not?"

"What I need from you and your people is nothing but the truth," Benny said again.

Benny did not possess the arrogance of a white man over a black man, Jay reflected. Perhaps human rights flowed in his blood.

With these words, Jay felt as if the first President of the country, Sir Seretse Khama had just woken up from the dead. Jay puffed hard on the cigarette and nodded several times, before tossing the butt aside. He remained silent. It was also a window of opportunity for Benny to observe something which had been troubling him.

There was this disturbing stark contrast of the residents of New Xade or former CKGR residents with that of their leaders, Benny observed when he turned his eyes to some residents who were murmuring near where he and Jay stood. Instead of the chubby faces he had seen from the leaders, the residents had tattooed tears and sunken cheeks like potholes in an abandoned road. They also had scars of pain etched on their faces. In fact, the Basarwa had the sadness of people mourning at the funeral of a dear relative, singing a song of death. Benny was jolted from observation by Phoko. The local lawyer glanced at his watch and motioned that the time set by the three judges for adjournment was over.

"Let's go inside the court."

They trod on the dusty sand soil led by Phoko and Benny while Jay and Jamana followed. The "courtroom" was essentially a classroom with red bricks that had been built for the new settlement, the new settlement being New Xade where relocated residents from the CKGR had been resettled. The three judges who wore bibs, gowns and for the lack of wigs, would have represented the complete picture of judges in a High Court session. Indeed the CKGR was God's wonder. It was true that the judges were actually there.

Benny and Phoko joined the state lawyers at the counsels' table while Jay and Jamana sat together among the audience. The court, or classroom, was fully packed.

A police officer exited through one of the doors, returning almost immediately like someone who had lost something. He closed the door and suddenly there was a bang!

"Court rise," said the police officer in the voice of a teacher asking students a question in class.

Judge Ditiro entered followed by Judge Brown and Judge Pamani. They bowed their heads before sitting on big chairs. Judge Ditiro adjusted his rimmed glasses which partly hid his red eyes. His hair was finely cut, his face dark. He looked at the audience before him the way a father would look at obedient and disobedient children.

Benny rose to his feet.

"My Lords," he said adjusting his long coat at the neck. "It is true that the first applicant, Mr. Jay Setlhare, represents the 242 applicants who are also former residents of the CKGR. He does so in his capacity as the leader of the First People of Kalahari." He then reverted to his seat.

"Yes Mr. Peolwane." Judge Ditiro addressed the lawyer representing the state.

Peolwane stood up, glanced at the three judges and Benny. He had a permanent smile that flickered now and then like a dying ember. Here and there, the lawyer's dark hair was dotted with tiny specks of grey. He had a long chin and his forehead was a little raised, assuring anyone who met him for the first time that this was one of the men with the best legal brains in the country.

"First of all, I must apologise for what happened last time," said Peolwane. "I had a feeling that the court wanted to embarrass me."

Pamani nodded and smiled, the smile of a pastor welcoming a backslidden member. "Apology accepted. We have no intention of sending anyone to jail. Again, it is not something that we enjoy. But at times circumstances dictate that, Mr. Peolwane."

The lawyer nodded and grinned shyly.

"Your worship," Peolwane raised his head from files which were smaller than Benny's. "We are of the view that the issue of Mr. Setlhare representing others was dealt with in the previous court session," he said. "Today we expected to hear something different. Anyway, we repeat our position that the application brought before you by the applicant, Mr. Jay Setlhare, is not properly before the court. We say that Mr. Setlhare does not have any legal right to launch an application on behalf of other former residents of the CKGR. We are going to demand affidavits from the other residents and we want them to file a fresh application. We will show the court why he cannot represent other residents later in our heads of arguments."

Judge Ditiro nodded.

"Mr. Benny any objection."

Benny shot up in time at the judge's words. "As the court pleases."

Now it was his turn to look at the three judges and then at Peolwane. But for effect, he also glanced at Phoko and then at the audience. He said he did not object to the argument raised by Peolwane, but stated that the court had to understand "a thing or two". The judges were clearly eager to know what the "one or two things" were as they nodded simultaneously. Like a Professor of Sociology, Benny lectured the court on the lifestyle of the Basarwa.

"We cannot deal with the relocation exercise without looking at the residents of the CKGR's way of life." It is said that at this point, those who had left their professional duties to attend the case murmured.

"Moving on My Lords," said Benny. "This case is to decide how the Basarwa want to live or how they choose to live." He paused and surveyed the audience as if looking for a voice to tell him that he was wrong. There was no one who was ready to challenge him or challenge him aloud anyway, so he continued. "In summary, this is about whether they choose to embrace development or civilization."

These words were to haunt Jay. They were the same words to be uttered by Judge Brown later: "Demanding dignity, respect. Our way of life may be different from those who have embraced civilization but you should respect it as much as you do with the kind of life that Adam and Eve led." How Jay had wanted to shake the judge's hand only to be stopped by the security guards at the Lobatse High Court Judge's Chambers.

Benny glanced at his court files now. "We would like to raise other points later when we file a new application and also respond to the question of the title deed that was raised by my learned friend in the previous session."

All of a sudden, there was unexpected uproar within the

audience. "The CKGR was given to us by God." Everyone's head turned towards the direction of the voice.

Standing like an imaginary snake that was said to have horns in folklore stories, was a man wearing eland horns and a fur jacket. His eyes blinked as if he was in shock, at the same time enjoying the pain he was being subjected to.

"Perhaps God is the one who has the title deed. You can ask your pastors to ask Him. I had expected something from the court but what I hear is irrelevant. Who is the government anyway? I would like to tell you what the gods have told me..."

This unexpected behaviour in court prompted Judge Ditiro to snap. "Mr. Setlhare, you might be a martyr but you should respect the court!"

Jay had now risen to his full height. "Even though I do not have the gowns or robes to show that I'm a lawyer, my people have chosen me to give them a voice, to look for and find them. I had thought the judges would help me find them, but I'm disappointed. I formed FPK in 1993 with the late Joseph Hirschfield," he said, ignoring the judge's warnings. "I do not need a piece of paper to show that the CKGR is my home."

Indeed those who had attended the court that day would have thought Jay's travelling across the world was an insult to the memories of the three chiefs who went to seek protection from Britain in 1885, for protection was granted and independence gained in 1966.

But this was Jay from the Kalahari Desert. He now walked out of the classroom, without even looking back. A police officer walked towards him.

"This matter has been postponed to December 12," said Judge Ditiro, his mind having lost interest in the court proceedings.

The police officer shouted again as soon as the judges

stood up. "Court rise." The three judges walked out of the classroom like university graduates wearing their gowns. People went outside.

"Now instead of focusing on national issues like HIV/AIDs or how our people can benefit from diamonds and sign another agreement with De Beers," said one man after the court session, "everyone wants to know what Jay is thinking or what he will tell the newspapers about his people as well as how he hates diamonds and development."

"True," said another. "His words have become our daily bread. But a bread that leaves the mouths of our leaders with a bitter taste."

But there were those who were also fascinated by Benny's grasp of the Basarwa case.

"How could a man come all the way from London and teach us, including our learned men and women, about the Basarwa, the very people we have been living with for many years? Does this mean that our sons and daughters went to schools across the sea for nothing?" they asked.

"It is certainly said that people hate things they do not understand," said a woman in her fifties. "We do not, and have never attempted, to understand the Basarwa."

Perhaps such comments about failing to put what one had learnt in school into practice would have pleased the Italian poet and philosopher Dante Alighieri, who once said that there is no need to have gone to school if you can't put what you have learnt into practice. But Judge Brown would, later in her judgment, mention something that would touch the hearts of many people; something that even Dante would have been proud of.

# Chapter Eight

The court had now moved to another new settlement, Kaudwane. After inspection, the court session started. It was held under a traditional shelter made of grass and sticks. Unlike at New Xade, there were only chairs but no tables, even for the three judges. After the three judges had taken their seats, a police officer stood up and announced: "Court is now in session."

Judge Brown focused her piercing eyes on Benny. "Mr. Benny, please advise your clients on how they should behave when they are in court."

Benny rose to his feet. "My Lady, the reason it seems my clients do not cooperate...," he paused, then continued, "is because they are not used to modern life, if one can speak in those terms. For instance, I have been told by my clients that an arrest is a provocation in the Basarwa culture." Benny paused again, deliberately for effect. It was the first time he had referred to or called his clients by their tribal name, Basarwa. "Secondly, they do not understand the relocation exercise. To them the relocation is like the way a tourist goes to another country, spends sometime there and returns. Or to be precise, the way Batswana in rural areas go to towns from their cattle posts and then go back home after doing whatever they went to do in town. In summary, my clients want to go back home."

Judge Brown nodded and smiled. "Okay, Mr. Benny for the sake of progress let's move onto other issues."

"My Lady, I would like to call my first witness.'" Benny glanced at the audience. "In fact, he is a symbol of my clients' lifestyle. This man, Morake, has been surviving on melons, roots and wild fruits," said Benny turning his eyes from Kwei Mae who was interpreting. But Peolwane shot up as if he had stumbled on live coals. "Objection!'

"Objection sustained," said Judge Ditiro. Peolwane's smile tugged at his cheeks, as he fiddled with a pen in his hand. He shook his head. "Our records show that Morake is a paid headman of arbitration for Molapo in New Xade." The three judges nodded their heads simultaneously. Benny rose to his feet. Turning to Peolwane he said, "But we agreed that we should not reveal too many details until the main arguments."

Peolwane sprang to his feet again. "I tried to warn you but you ignored that advice."

"Counsels," said Judge Ditiro, "I'm going to postpone this matter to tomorrow. You should learn to handle yourselves like officers of the court not like the applicants themselves." With these words, the three judges walked out of the classroom.

Jay walked out of the court followed by Jamana and reporters. Phoko emerged from another door accompanied by Benny. As usual, the British lawyer wore long robes like that of the pope. With his glasses perched on his nose, Jay had thought Benny would remind him of Drum of Kuru Development Trust. But he did not. "Are you saying we cannot go back home?" Jay asked, thinking about how he would locate his missing people.

Benny shook his head. "I have to look at how the relationship between your people and the government used to be like." He ran his hand across his face while the other held some documents. "I mean before the relocation or even just after independence." He shook his head several times. "I will have to go through a report that was produced by a South African ecologist. He will testify in the case."

Jay shielded his eyes from the rising sun and said, "we

believe that there are international companies that are going to team up with the authorities to steal our land and our highly valued treasures."

Benny nodded, then he shrugged.

"Mr. Jay?" The frown turned into a smile when the lawyer saw panic on Jay's face. "Many people from all over the world will come and testify. Some will be interested in your lifestyle. In other words, what is so special about CKGR?"

Jay nodded and his eyes lit up. "When these multinational companies come here, they control the minerals of the country." Jay blinked. "The authorities get drunk and forget about their own people. The country belongs to a few and their international friends."

Benny nodded too, more than before. "Is that why you hate civilization and development?" The sympathy that Benny had felt doing his thesis was now focused on the Basarwa. He had to rescue them. Jay had told him that his people were equivalent to human rubbish, if ever there was such. And Benny agreed.

"Everyone has a purpose in life," said Benny. "Judges protect those wronged. Lawyers protect those who commit wrongs and those who also find themselves as victims of others actions. Police arrest criminals. Everybody has rights, without rights there can be no life."

"But you and those judges, can you help me find my people, even if they are not shining or worth it like diamonds?"

At that moment Jamana turned his back on Benny. He shook his head towards Jay.

"The case has been dismissed."

Jay shook his head too, but in shock. "What?" Their conversation did not require interpretation into English for the British lawyer. He switched his eyes between Jamana and Jay. Benny's sympathetic eyes that had brought new hope to Jay, were now on Jay. Jay had also thought those sympathetic eyes reminded him of the first President, Sir Seretse Khama when he had visited the CKGR. Perhaps the first President would have understood. Was he not a human rights activist himself after being persecuted for marrying a white woman? But what had Seretse done?

Jay wondered. He married the woman despite hatred from the Boers from South Africa and the fact that they called some of their dogs by his name as way of dissuading him. Instead, he had told them to go and call their dogs with their mothers' names. To his people in Serowe, the former President, who was also the Paramount chief, told them that in each family there should be people of different kinds, those who destroy and those who build and bring changes. This reflection brought a sense of hope to Jay and he laughed discretely. But as he turned his eyes from Jamana to the lawyer, he felt as if Benny's eyes were actually cold, as if he did not care, or so Jay thought guiltily. Perhaps Jay should lose trust and have no confidence in the lawyer. Jay's eyes narrowed. When Jamana had explained what the dismissal of the case meant, Jay stood there quiet, his eyes immobile. He followed Jamana to the van, with Benny in tow. In the van, Jay had expected anger and frustration from the lawyer; however Benny simply grinned, showing his cream white teeth.

"We will have to start afresh."

Jay nodded and then shook his head as if confused. Benny observed that Jay placed the relocation of his people at par with the genocide of the Jews during the reign of the Nazi dictator, Adolf Hitler. He never understood why and did not bother to ask.

Jay's upper lip twisted. Phoko only listened while Jamana interpreted to Jay as Benny spoke. Those who had never acknowledged the presence of Jay's people nodded when they met him outside court. The reporters were waiting anxiously to pounce on him. It was like he had killed a president, Jamana was to tell him later.

"We need more protection," he told Benny.

Benny turned to Phoko, then to Jamana. "Tell Jay once again that he should not talk to the newspaper people."

Phoko nodded and blinked rapidly. "Yes, about the case before the court."

Jamana nodded in unison. "I did tell him, but we cannot wait to go back home."

Jay looked at Benny and wondered if he should have hope. If he had any racial discrimination, Jay observed, Benny did not show it.

Jamana scratched his head and spoke up. "Jay said that I should tell you that if someone does anything or something considered unacceptable, it is always associated with our people. And he can't wait to share the secret that the authorities have been hiding from the rest of the world."

Benny's eyes glistened as though he had been waiting to hear just that.

"But what you say to the papers might be used against our court application."

Jamana smiled and nodded. "Well, we should not lose hope. After all Mandela said the walk to freedom is very long."

Facing the sun, Benny's eyes started to water. "I nearly forgot to ask something, out of curiosity. Why don't you have confidence in the local human rights organizations?"

The answer shot from Jamana's lips as if it had been always at the ready. "Because they benefit from the system. Anything that might suggest why we are relocated is kept secret."

"Yes, I have gone through the report done by the South

African ecologist; it said you can coexist with wild animals."

"You cannot find the information as to why we were relocated."

Benny nodded and then shrugged. "Perhaps it is with multinational companies as you said earlier on."

Jay smiled with a pained grin, like someone emerging from a dental operation. "We never had any meaningful relationship with the local organizations," Jay said. "If that is what you were asking me. The local organizations only write in newspapers. They do not act. In fact, our organization, First People of Kalahari, is the best so far."

Jamana nodded before he smiled. "That is true."

"But would you say the relocation is related to minerals?" Benny asked.

Jay swallowed hot saliva. "All over the country, the relationship of my people and authorities has been that of slaves and kings." Jamana nodded again and this time his face looked sad. "And we are not going to allow people to stay in the new settlements."

Benny's eyes bulged. "Oh I see."

"But can you help us go back home?"Jay stroked his beard. "Perhaps if we say that we are being relocated as a result of a mineral discovery."

There was silence.

Benny turned his eyes away from the shining sun. "Maybe, maybe not."

"We cannot stand this place," Jay said shaking his head. "We know what will happen if we do not find the missing people and their stolen land. I and they would not last. We could not."

Benny, who had been sitting in the passenger seat of the van, rose to his feet.

"Jay..."

"You are just like them," Jay said. "You do not understand. Do you?"

"But you...like who?"

"The authorities. Didn't you go to the same schools?"

"Jay..."

"If they do not let us go back home," Jay said, "we will do something never done before." That terrible comparison to the Jews during Hitler's rule was evidently on Jay's mind again. What was it that this man loved so much in the desert, the British lawyer wondered as Jay walked away from the van.

Jay pointed a finger at Benny. "Remember that a man is never afraid to lose his voice when fighting over the eland of his forefathers."

"Oh, is that why you are wearing horns?" asked Benny

"No, it is a manner of speaking," said Jamana. "It means that if one has a rightful claim over something, he should never give up in spite of the hurdles he encounters."

"But why is it that the eland is so important to your people, Jamana?"

"You will learn as you mingle with our people. The eland is the most prized animal to us as much as diamonds are the most precious item to people in the Western world and their friends here in this country."

Jamana broke into tears, preventing Benny from asking further questions. Without a word, Jamana motioned goodbye with his head, joined Jay in the van and drove off. Benny shook his head, saddened by the conditions his clients found themselves in. He too joined Phoko in his BMW and the two drove off in silence, each thinking how to convince Jay not talk to the newspapers and other organizations.

# Chapter Nine

It was a feeling of content that made Jay enter the van quicker than he would have. But the shrubs, sand dunes and the savannah bush veldt seemed to understand what he lacked. Jay and Jamana were on the road to Gaborone, after Jay's quarrel with their lawyer and also after he disrupted a meeting held by government officials in New Xade. Now he wanted to go to Gaborone and search for some of his people there.

The journey back to the big city was longer than it had seemed when he and Jamana came to New Xade.

Jamana turned his eyes from the road ahead to Jay.

"What will the other citizens say when they learn about this?"

But Jay remained silent, for he could also not believe what he was going through. It seemed he was fighting an argument in his heart. Jamana glanced at the road, before turning his eyes to Jay again, hoping to get an answer. For a moment, Jamana felt like running away from the vehicle he was in, from the CKGR, from Jay, just go to Gaborone and look for a job.

But when it was his turn to look at Jamana, Jay smiled. In fact, he laughed and his eyes assured Jamana. After all, they were humans. The humiliation they had suffered at the hands of the superiors! That was an unspeakable abomination.

Jamana negotiated the curves as the road was damaged by the big trucks that ferried tourists. After hours of driving, Jamana put the vehicle into parking gear.

He patted a sleeping Jay on the shoulder. "We have arrived," he said.

Jay rubbed his eyes, opened the door and jumped out. Reporters shouted out his name. He remembered that he was not supposed to talk to reporters. Without warning, Jay re-entered the van and motioned to Jamana that they should drive off. They passed through well decorated buildings, took a turn to the left, and passed in front of the Attorney General Chambers and the Ministry of Health. Eventually, Jay and Jamana's van pulled up at Cresta Lodge.

"These days, people fall in love at a young age," said Jamana, coming out of the van. He pointed at a young couple across the road and Jay looked at him.

"Haven't you heard?" Jay asked. His crocodile-like smile was back on his face.

"That boy, like others elsewhere in this country, is preparing that little girl for elderly men whose aging skin has been polished into youth by money just as a diamond sorter would polish a rough diamond into an appealing necklace." Jamana nodded, but said nothing. He was deep in thoughts as if the young couple reminded him of his days at school.

"But these rich men are cruel," said Jay. "They are enemies of condoms and they sleep with these young girls without using even one. They talk about leading the nation in the prevention of AIDS while they are the ones who make the young girls their mattresses. Anyway, people are not what they preach," he paused momentarily.

"You know what?" he continued "It's like the question I was asked last time. I was asked to prove if indeed I was married to my wives. But remember that it is not in our culture to oppress ourselves with metals called rings around our fingers. I had to also tell those civilized men and women that we also do not mark graves in the CKGR, but bury our dead near a particular tree. These are some of the things that have brought me here today. To tell the negotiating team that unless we are told the truth about the relocation I have no choice but to take you back home. Because if we keep on being asked such questions, it's a sign that problems are on their way to attack our simple, inexpensive lifestyle." Jamana remained silent. Then the smile on Jay's face developed into a chuckle.

"You know," he said turning to Jamana. Their eyes met like old lovers. "Last time you did not tell me what exactly happened to Peolwane. Is it true he was locked up in prison the day I walked out of the court?"

Jamana nodded and smiled mischievously. "You know, he cried like a little child."

"But why?"

"He said Judge Brown did not like him and what she wanted was to see him in jail."

The chuckle now turned into a smile again. "What really happened?"

"He said he was given only three hours to prepare his application after being locked up. He said what Judge Brown wanted was to humiliate him."

"But why would she?" Jay's eyes shone like a star in the Kalahari's dark sky. "I mean what were the circumstances that led to his arrest?"

"You know Peolwane had made a request for the case to be adjourned three times but there was no response from the judges."

"Oh I see, but why was he asking for that?"

"That was exactly what Judge Pamani had asked him, only for him to say it was private."

Jay shook his head.

Now it was Jamana's turn to chuckle, revealing protruding teeth. "Pamani wanted to explain something to him but Judge Brown took over and asked Peolwane to stand up and he refused."

"Did he?"

"Yes he did," said Jamana with a smile that indicated triumph. "I have never seen such power in a woman. Though her body had seemed lost in those gowns, there is judicial power beneath them. She just ordered police to arrest Peolwane and he took to his heels and fled in a car."

Jay giggled, turning his eyes to look through the window. "Yes, it serves him right."

He nodded several times. "People think I wear these horns for nothing."

"What really happened is that Peolwane was trying to secure a witness from America," said Jamana. "Her name is Florence Smith and he wanted to find out about her research in the CKGR and if she had found dead animals... and you know... when she went there in July. Judge Ditiro said some of the questions were inadmissible in court. Later Peolwane asked for adjournment without standing up. Judge Brown then said he should be locked up for four days for refusing to stand up when told to do so by the judges. The next day he wanted to bring state lawyers to represent him, but Judge Brown told him that he should hire his own private lawyers. It was my first time to see a big man being reduced to a mere boy by a woman."

There was silence.

Jay shrugged his shoulders. "I think it can happen that something beneath a lawyer's trousers can forbid him from standing up. Even you, you would not. Just imagine how you would face the judges with something sticking out like an arrow in a bow ready to fly."

Jamana giggled and wiped his face with the back of his

hand. "To show that Peolwane was just like me and you, a different judge, Marang Mothathedi appeared in shorts, wearing a T-shirt with a loose neck like a street child that I once saw at a Gaborone land fill. And indeed the judge said Peolwane had disrespected court."

Jay burst out laughing. He stepped out of the van and glanced at Jamana.

"Lets call off this meeting," said Jamana unexpectedly, but Jay did not answer. He entered the lodge.

Sitting at the reception was a young, buxom lady, who forced a smile when she saw Jay and Jamana enter.

"Hey, this is not a meeting for herd boys. It is for important guests." She assessed Jay up and down as if weighing his status in the society. "Or do you think this is a government department to receive handouts?"

The insult did not anger Jay. In fact, everywhere he went, he expected it from people who were different from his own people, those who were not from his kind. Or those who did not know who he was.

"Please go outside at once."

"I'm here to attend the Ditshwanelo meeting."

"Oh are you Jay Setlhare?"

Jay nodded.

"Oh that's you." The young woman knelt down such that her large bosom nearly touched the floor. She was overcome with guilt for having spoken ill of a man who everyone wanted to shake hands with these days. "I thought..." Her voice trailed off.

Jay only nodded.

"Good day. Oh you are here for the Ditshwanelo centre for Human Rights Seminar?"

Jay nodded again, adding, "yes."

The young lady raised her hand and pointed at one of the doors adjacent to the entrance that Jay had used. Jay walked towards a room with a door marked: Conference Room, with Jamana following behind him. As soon the two got seated, there was a gentle knock at the door.

Meaningful glances were exchanged. Jamana and Jay seemed to be asking themselves the same question: Are we worthy enough to be negotiating for the people of CKGR?

"Come in," Jay said to Jamana, without taking away his eyes from the door.

Delegates filled the room littered with note books. General greetings were exchanged and the delegates sat at a table separate to where Jamana and Jay sat.

Jamana picked up a few fastened papers from handed them over to the delegates. He examined the documents, resting his head on his hand.

In front of him, the memory of the incident in New Xade was revived. Instead of the papers before him, Jay only visualized officials "armed" with sweets and blankets handing these over to the residents. But his people had rallied behind him, forcing the senior officials and their entourage to wonder at Jay's power. Was it because of the eland horns?

The papers fell from his unsteady hands and delegates peered at them curiously like a treasure. Marked on the pages were the words: Jay Setlhare and 242 Others versus... Registered at The Lobatse High On This Date of...

The delegates looked at each other. So it was true. The delegates wanted to ask Jay many questions; why had he disrupted meetings held by the authorities, the truth about the relocation.... But the delegates should have listened when Jay spoke to his people in New Xade that painful morning, before coming to Gaborone to the meeting. At first, Jay had not wanted to look into the eyes of the officials in New Xade. He had just looked vaguely at the shrubs, savannah bush veldt and addressed his ancestors. When he did look into the delegation's eyes it was an omen. He wanted an explanation as to what had really transpired before he could disrupt the meeting.

"We want you to start a new life," one of the senior officials had said to the people before Jay's arrival. But the residents of the new settlement, New Xade, south ofthe CKGR did not reply. Their silence was ominous. For an answer, they just sat silently with chins resting between their palms.

"We know we could have done this," said the same senior official and paused as if he was not sure of his words, his actions. "Basarwa, we are here to…" Indeed the whole explanation seemed unreal, words from somewhere else, or falsehoods. "I mean after independence. But it was those who created the reserve who…" But the turning of the residents' heads towards the south disturbed the senior official's lecture. He did not glance at Jay, it seemed he had not heard or seen him. Or Jay's existence or presence there meant nothing to him. So the official continued, "we will…"

Jay coughed. The silent cries of his people pricked him like a poisoned arrow sliding into the behind of a young and fragile eland.

"I say disperse at once," he told those who had gathered at the meeting. "If you want to go back home, disperse now. Or I will stop telling the truth as to why we have to go home." Women whose babies had been resting on their laps clutched their skirts. There was an element of fear and pride on their faces. For the first time they followed instructions, hearing the voice of one of their own. Was it true that Jay was from the CKGR, the government officials wondered. But there was no one to answer their question because the people had dispersed. By the time the senior officer turned his eyes to look at Jay, he was gone.

Now at Cresta Lodge, many organizations had come for

the meeting organized by Ditshwanelo, churches, and other organizations that called themselves the negotiating team. Jay and Jamana represented the FPK, together with three other members from FPK. The meeting took the whole day. Reporters were told that the meeting was confidential and they would be briefed on what transpired later.

As they exited the Lodge, Jay shook his head several times as if he had discovered an unexpected truth. He glanced at Jamana, then looked away.

"If I meet the reporters or the authorities now I will tell them that I have changed," he said. "That is, I support the relocation now. I have also stopped looking for my lost people. I would rather look for diamonds." Jamana only bowed and shook his head, shocked. "Do you mean that we are no longer going to Britain to meet the Members of Parliament there and tell them our story?" asked Jamana.

"Oh, I nearly forgot," Jay said wiping at his eyes. "We are going there tomorrow to look for my people."

# Chapter Ten

"What is this we hear?" asked the Member of Parliament, Peter Charles. He was the MP for Liberal Democratic from the House of Commons in Britain. That was when they first learnt the story. Sitting in his parliamentary office in downtown London, waiting for a Survival International representative, his curiosity grew.

"Or should I say, are there still such people?" He looked at another MP, Chamberlain Grey who chaired the All Parliamentary Group for Tribal People.

"That is the question that is on everybody's lips," said Grey without looking at the other MP.

"The question is, is it true that there are people in the Kalahari who are resisting development and civilization?"

"I have heard strange stories before," said Charles looking outside the window of his office. "But never before have I heard of a heresy like this. You know, in the olden days our grandfathers would burn such rebels at the stake."

"Yes that is so," agreed Grey placing one leg over the other. "But let's not call it heresy. Different people have different beliefs and cultures. Again, let's not make conclusions before we learn the whole story."

Grey's philosophy in life was that everybody should be equal. This, he had learnt while a member of the Catholic Church, which he had been in since he was in his mother's womb. His mother, so people said, was a true Christian who placed her faith before everything else. So Grey was like a missionary.

"I have no idea how the Basarwa live," said Charles,

looking away from Grey. "I only read about their lifestyle when I was at school. I suppose there is no need to relocate them. After all, they live a nomadic lifestyle. They will move to another place without being told to do so."

"Not exactly," said Rose from Survival International who had just joined the two MPs. "You know it is not that they are nomadic. They only move when there is a war or when there is no food where they are staying. But the reserve, CKGR, is full of wild animals, wild fruits."

"Now that is very interesting," said Charles looking at Rose with revived interest, his eyes glowing like neon lights.

"So what if there are minerals discovered there? You know that Botswana's minerals are very secretive, if one can speak in those terms. Even during our colonization of that country, we just dismissed it as a desert. We benefited nothing from colonizing that country."

"I understand the Basarwa have been a very friendly and peaceful people," said Grey in his sympathetic way.

Rose sat facing the two MPs. She wore a black suit and had a small frame but her eyes made her look more powerful than her figure.

"Yes," she said, a pen in one hand. She raised her head from the paper on which she was taking notes.

"They are harmless, you can say. Even a quarrel among themselves is an offence."

There was silence for a while.

"But why is it that now they are opposing the relocation if they are what you say they are?" persisted Charles in an inquisitive manner. "I mean, if you say they are a peaceful people, they must be obedient as well."

"They fear that they will be integrated," said Rose wrinkling her nose. "The magnificent and ancient world of the Kalahari would come to an end."

"But I can't make head or tail of the whole thing," said Charles unable to hide his contempt for the subject anymore. As expected, when he adopted that sullen mood his face grew pale.

"Those people need us most," Rose said. "In fact, to be precise, we need the support of the whole world. If you have mingled with the Basarwa a little, you would understand and perhaps change your attitude towards."

This sudden accusation did not go down well with Charles. His face changed from pale to red.

"What do you mean?" he asked. "It's not that I have an attitude. We, the British, have to account for what is happening in that country. If history comes back to haunt people there, and is a consequence of our colonization, we shouldn't hide in our palaces. Don't think that your organization knows more than we do. My attitude, or let me say the British's attitude, is that things should be done transparently. Let the authorities there handle this issue as long as they consult with their people and seek our help where necessary. If, for instance, they need our assistance explaining how and why CKGR was created, we will help." Rose looked at the MP with a stern face.

"Is it not our civilization that has done more harm to Africans than good?" she asked.

"But ..." stammered Grey. "But ... don't you think that authorities there would say you are meddling into the affairs of their own country?" Grey always stammered when expressing something that touched his heart. With his chin between his palms, his eyes blinked rapidly.

"We know everything," said Rose her voice raised higher.

"We met with the authorities there in 1989 over the first relocation. As an old Human Rights organization we know how to tackle these things. We believe that local organizations there and some authorities themselves do not understand the impact of the relocation. We are there to guide them. The relocation of 2002 would not have happened had we been involved. But the organizations there folded their arms. That is why we thought of bypassing them and going straight to the Basarwa. We want to help the Basarwa feel that they are also important people and that they have always been important. Their lifestyle is their own civilization and development that we so cherish. In a nutshell, we want to help them restore their dignity. We want to put them not only on the map of their country, but also on the world map. We are there to bring change. Say, for instance, there is mining where they stay; we want them to be in control."

"But still I don't understand," said Charles turning his eyes from Rose to Grey.

"They care more about animals and fruits than anything else. To them, wild animals and wild fruits are more important than diamonds, I'm told. Anyway, I think we have to visit CKGR on a fact-finding mission."

"Yes, we have been invited to go there," said Grey.

"We have to meet the ancient people," said Charles.

"I have learnt that some of them wear horns just as you and I would wear hats. What a miracle lies ahead!"

Rose stood up, slung her handbag and made ready to leave. But it was a knock on the door that made her freeze. She turned her eyes at the same time with the two MPs.

"Come in please," said Charles. The door opened. Standing at the door was someone that Rose recognized as Seven Garry. He was flanked by none other than Jay and Jamana. Jay raised his eyebrows as if he recognized the two MPs more than he did Rose. He even smiled. But the hosts were lost for words. Who could this man be? In response, Jay raised a placard with the following message inscribed on it: *Can you help me find my people and go back home?*

# Chapter Eleven

Back in Botswana. Just as they were about to enter the van, the terrifying mood of the day before was revived. No sooner had he sat in the front seat than they came for him. Now they were led by others from outside the country. They were about 15, or so he counted. He held out his five fingers, three times each and stopped. They had been waiting for him. But he had to defend his home come what may. The memory of the wildlife officials, whips cutting his face, shoulders and across the eyes brought pain and he felt de-energised as the fifteen people approached him. The approach of these strangers made the memory of the wildlife officials turn into something real. He could see the wildlife officials instead of these 15 strangers; the wooden part of a gun knocking him to the ground as a punch hit his groin.

Again, the memory of blood spurting out of his nostrils, his eyes, brought nausea and dizziness. In an effort to drive away this unwanted feeling, he searched for his bow and arrows only to remember that he had just descended from a plane from Britain. Remembering the promises of the British MPs, that they would be in the country soon to help him find his people, Jay held his head up.

In Botswana, there were those who still looked him up and down. Was this not an old man who was visibly deep in thoughts as to how to look for the stray cattle of rich Batswana.

But still the reporters followed him as he and Jamana passed by the garages which sold Japanese and Singapore second-hand cars in Mogoditshane. His eyes were blinded by the illuminated bodies of thousands of cars.

Across the road were stalls where people sold orange fruits and many other items. They passed the Total Filling station and Jay peeped through the window to throw away a cigarette butt.

On his right were slums which he had seen there as long as he could remember.

Then suddenly, as the reporters kept on pestering him, he remembered that a few years earlier some politicians had been suspended from office after they were allegedly involved in land scandals. He shuddered to think of such a thing happening to the CKGR. The thought aroused the anger he had felt when he was arrested and beaten while trying to enter his home, the CKGR. The questions from reporters also increased his agitation. What had people in Mogoditshane done to protect their land when they were told to vacate it while the politicians who had stolen land were again rewarded with other posts? Nothing.

Jay had made up his mind now. He resolutely refused to let fear or any beating or weapons subdue his will, his dream to repossess the CKGR. He had to conquer. He could not fail his people. Neither could he let reporters confuse him, no matter how knowledgeable they were. The pleading and insistent voices of his people reached him instantly: *Going Back To CKGR*. He told Jamana to stop the van. He jumped out and hurried down Haile Selassie Avenue.

0-0-0-0-0

Suddenly, Jay was transported to his visit in London. That was before he had met the two MPs, Peter Charles and Chamberlain Grey, as well as before Rose and Seven Garry of Survival International. That was also when he could visualize his position in society as his future unfurled before him. He had pictured all the positions in the society. How could he not do so when he had had the privilege of meeting the British Prince.

"We are voices sent to talk to you from the CKGR," the leader of the group, Hirschfield had said. The Prince did not answer at once. Jay was among the men that the Prince surveyed with his eyes, unable to speak. Their half closed eyes demanded the Prince's opinion on the CKGR.

"We are here to see you," Jay added as if to add some weight to Hirschfield's words.

"Oh," said the Prince at last as if waking up from a dream. "I see." He was momentarily in deep thoughts. Then he looked in the direction of another room adjacent to the door marked, Leisure Room.

"Lucky, bring something for these visitors, they are from a far off place…"

Hirschfield nodded many times. "CKGR is the name." There was pride in his voice as if he spoke of a hero that he admired and was well known all over the world.

A man in white clothes emerged from another room. To Jay, the man looked like a nurse. He had on his head a coned cloth, a fez. An apron also hung loosely from his neck down to his knees. It was when he had served them with drinks that Jay realized that the man was a steward. Jay had seen such clothes being worn by cooks working in expensive restaurants when he had gone to the USA to canvass support for a return to the CKGR.

"We want you to step in," said Hirschfield as his hand lifted the drink from the table, looking the Prince in the eye.

"We want you to tell them, rather remind the authorities in our country that the land belongs to us. How can they forget so soon? I mean, from independence in

1966 to 2002, or to be precise 1987 when they wanted to evict our people?"

"I was wondering," the Prince said still trying to calm himself. "What could have made you travel from Kalahari to this far off place?" The four men shook their heads as if they had seen the medicine to a disease that was said to be beyond healing, the first of its kind in the CKGR and the entire Kalahari Desert.

This reassured them that he was there for them as he also nodded his head.

"I mean, if there is democracy in South Africa, unlike in the past when the threats of invasion from white farmers and miners saw the three chiefs coming here to seek protection," said the Prince also remembering the first President's marriage to a British woman which some whites in South Africa could not entertain. By then the House of Commons, as the British Parliament is called, he remembered, was facing outside pressure and it was keen to avoid upsetting South Africa's national government which was about to introduce apartheid.

"Perhaps it is because we were not represented then." Hirschfield cut the Prince off as he raised his eyes from the Mahogany table.

The great man whose blood flowed with royalty was startled by the other's voice. It demanded sympathy, the voice of Hirschfield.

"We, of the CKGR, want to go back home," added Hirschfield ignoring the shock on the Prince's face.

"That is our home. You will remember that during the times of Sir Charles Warren who ensured that the Bechuanaland Protectorate materialized in 1885, it was agreed that the place should be our home."

There was silence. The Prince coughed. His four visitors looked at him at the same time. He sat on an expensive revolving armchair. Unlike when he was in the CKGR wearing a safari suit, that day he had on a dark three piece suit which Jay thought made him more light skinned than when he had first met him in the CKGR.

His pen was hovering over his mouth. Jay wondered if he could master use of his left hand as he shifted his eyes from the Prince to the floor, which was covered with an expensive shiny red carpet decorated with flowers of different kinds. To Jay, such a carpet could have attracted bees were it in the CKGR. The chambers, Jay observed, were cosy and cool. There was a persistent draught from somewhere, which, as he reflected later, could keep the heat and the bees at bay were they to be attracted. He also learned that it was called an air conditioner. If only they could have such things in the CKGR where it was really hot, he thought.

The sofas they sat on were black and gleaming while the chambers' interior was made of mahogany.

"It cannot happen in such a country," the Prince said as an afterthought.

"We have been to America, to China, to Russia, France and that is what everybody is saying; it cannot happen," said Hirschfield with his hands in the air as if swearing by his ancestors.

"Some people in other parts of the country have been consulted when evicted, why not us?"

The Prince did not answer again. He appeared absorbed as his eyes surveyed the tile floor.

"What we would like to know is," added Jay. "Did the authorities consult you? Because they did not consult us." At these words, the Prince was touched, for he only shook his head and stared ahead. He nodded several times like someone who had discovered an unexpected secret, a truth.

"Did they not mention anything to the effect that there will be mining in our ancestral land?" Jay asked, again his eyes shrinking and his mind wandering to his days as a mine worker in South Africa where some people were said to have lost land to big international companies. Again the Prince only shook his head and looked away as if hiding something from his visitors.

"We are not moving out," repeated Jay. The Prince coughed again. It was an indication that he had something to say. And he did.

"What will the authorities of your country say if they learnt that you are here?" The Prince asked at last.

"We do not care," said Hirschfield throwing his arms in the air. "They don't care about us."

The Prince nearly asked if the CKGR was not a God forsaken place. But even the royal blood flowing in his veins could not help him ask the question. Rather, he felt sorry for the four contorted faces before him. He only asked, "Is that so?"

Perhaps that was the result of the wrong policies of our colonial administration; he nearly added but thought better of it.

"We want you to lobby the British government to help us find our lost people."

With these words, Jay also wondered if he really was in Britain. The sun had seemed to have set in different directions reminding Jay of a feeling he had as a little boy when driving in a car. Trees would retreat in the opposite direction. Were they really in England?

"I think we have met before," the Prince said, directing his words to Hirschfield and Jay as if he had discovered the unexpected truth he had been looking for.

"That was in 1987 in CKGR, during the most entertaining dance I have never seen, the trance Dance."

0-0-0-0-0

Jay was now shaken out of his daydream again by one of the reporters stepping on his shoes.

"I'm sorry I stepped on you Mr. Jay."

Jay coughed. He almost started speaking, to tell them

that he supported the relocation, or share with them what he had discussed with the British MPs while in London. But he stopped, remembering the words of the first president of the country, "A people without a culture are a lost nation." He rubbed his eyes.

Expecting his lips to part immediately, the reporters waited for him to answer. He took his cigarette away from his lips. Indeed he was a worried man. He waited for the smoke to curl away lazily, but said nothing in response to the questions. Some of the journalists were from America, Britain, South Africa, Germany, China, and France. Perhaps only journalists from other planets such as Mars, Venus and the like were not there. The CKGR had brought people from all over the world. Some to testify what they knew about it, how the British, during their colonization of Botswana founded the CKGR, the purpose of the reserve and so on. On the other hand, journalists wanted information to inform those in other parts of the world who did not know. But they would soon know.

The enthusiasm that the reporters had welcomed Jay with died prematurely as Jay refused to field their questions. It was replaced with frustration, disappointment and hopelessness. Why did Jay not field questions from them? Some local journalists backed off. Jay only thought of locating his people and going back home, even if he had to engage in a battle with soldiers and armed police! Nevertheless, he had instantly become a man of substance; the person of the moment. Every gesture, not only his words, was news for the newspapers, radios, televisions and word of mouth. From that day, through the news from various radio stations, newspapers, televisions and word of mouth, Jay had become the terror of the authorities.

But the question remained: why did he not want to talk? What was he hiding? Rumour had it that when he stepped on the ground, it jingled instead of shook.

But what was clear was that Jay wanted the CKGR more than anything in life. But why was he opposing the relocation? Did he have any intention of going back to the CKGR and wearing a loincloth? Would he not miss wining and dining with kings and queens, and the five-star hotels. Would he exchange this lifestyle for hunting and gathering? Who was he? What exactly did he want to achieve? Did he really want to stay in the dry desert?

The thought that the British Prince was on the side of his people brought a smile on Jay's face. And the authorities thought they had done something by employing his people at the cattle posts he reflected now as he did later. They had the audacity, in fact the bitter sense of humour, to call that a step towards development. Jay reflected again, now with bitterness. He had to rescue his people, those at the cattle posts and those in prisons who had broken laws they did not understand. He would lead all the leaders in Europe to find his people and go home. But to destroy the image of the country as some people warned him, seemed a crime bigger than hunting without a license in the reserve, Jay reflected, as an icy liquid settled in his stomach. This sudden change of deviating from rebellion shocked and numbed him. Suddenly, he hated himself for asking these questions. He wished the questions would not have come to mind. But the questions came despite his wishes, his wishing of not thinking about the consequences of urging the people to go back home. But the thought that there had never been a person who could make change among his people inflamed him, so strangely that, he nearly laughed.

The prospects of bringing change among his people brought an urge to call his people that instant and go back to the reserve. He wanted to shout. But he only managed to whisper. It was a call: his people's voices.

The reporters were still there. But he could not answer them right away. At long last there was an unclear sound in his throat. What the reporters could get as they stumbled on each other, still waiting for answers was only, "Oh CKGR... Oh CKGR."

Jay shrugged to indicate that he did not see them, did not hear what they were saying. Instead he saw short people, like him, with dishevelled hair, wearing nothing but loincloths, beads around their necks, bare footed, sad faces and light skinned.

Suddenly, it started to rain. It had at first started as a drizzle but now it washed away Jay's tears, for he understood its sympathy as he refused to shelter under the roofs of shops, as the reporters hurried to do.

Thoughts of telling the reporters that he had agreed to negotiate with the authorities, his discussions with the British MPs, dispersed. Perhaps he had forgotten so soon that the land had been taken already, he reflected. What would he be negotiating for? Tears long suppressed since the beating and arrest by wildlife officials flowed as he hurried back to Jamana at the filing station. He went out into the rain, possessed by the desire to share with Jamana what he had told the reporters.

# Chapter Twelve

With a deeply wrinkled face, Jay looked away as soon as he found Jamana in the van.

"I told them that just like their own kind, they did not care about us."

Jamana shook his head. "But Jay, did Benny not warn you against talking to the newspaper people? Even the judges told you that we should not talk to those people."

"We have no choice but to seek help from Survival International and the British MPs," said Jay without emotion. Jamana could not see the worry as it was growing dark.

He now looked Jamana in the eye.

"Did I not run around the courts, government departments, schools and even at their cattle posts asking the authorities to let my people go home? Jamana tell me."

He paused.

"None of them were willing to give me permission to go home. Every time my people want to go home, they have to ask for permission. Just like the blacks in South Africa during apartheid. I know that from experience. While working at the mine there, we always had to be in possession of permits. I never thought such a thing could happen here. But here I am, stuck. It is true that the hearth stone at a place you visited may also be there at your mother's hut when you return. And I'm accused of being unpatriotic, of breaking the law, only because I told Survival International the same story that people here did not want to hear. They say the security agents must take me to task. Let me tell you Jamana, when I ask if anyone has seen my people, the answer I get is that they have only seen diamonds, my people are invisible because they are not shining. But I will never sleep until I find my people."

"Jay, what did you tell the newspaper people then?" Jamana's voice was strained as if he pitied Jay for having tampered with a certain section of the law.

"I told them that it is a lie," Jay said looking outside the window of the van. "It's a lie that Survival International speaks for us. It is I who tells them what to tell the world. I told the reporters how I arrived from a hunting expedition to find that my wives and my people had been stolen."

"Did they ask you some other questions?"

"Yes they did."

Jay looked at Jamana's face as if he was sensing betrayal of the struggle. "They asked me if abductions of powerless people still exist." He paused again to see how Jamana would react. But the other man was staring ahead, eyes on the road as they returned to New Xade. Jay continued speaking. "I told the newspaper people that the SAMI tribe of Norway, the Basarwa from Namibia and South Africa want to hear me speak. They want the world to hear our voice for the first time. They must know that we are not mute, that we are visible and that they should not only see diamonds."

Jamana nodded and coughed. "But I have a feeling that if we continue giving interviews to newspaper people we may lose the case at the High Court."

Jay chuckled. It was the chuckle of a mad man laughing without a cause.

"Do you mean we have to keep quiet whilst we are barred from going back home, when other people sleep at their homes?"

"No...I mean there are channels to follow."

"Like what?"

"Like waiting for the case to resume in the court."

"Jamana, didn't you see that Peolwane had adopted delaying tactics. He knows that we have no money and the case will end up being removed from the court roll, as you call it, and perhaps lose the chance to find my people."

"But...but..."

"I'm too tired of hearing but... but." Jay's creased face resembled the channels of the Okavango Delta. "Remember that I was supposed to talk to one of the leaders last time on how best we can find a long lasting solution to go back home. But she only asked me about my mating habits instead of telling me how I could find my people, make them visible and go home. To her, it was as if I were a different creature, different from mankind. I do not know if she wanted to experience it with me, but because I was preoccupied with going back home, I didn't tell her my mind."

Jamana looked at him and shook his head. "Is that what you told the newspaper people?"

Jay raised an eyebrow and lit a cigarette. His eyes narrowed and his cheek bones stood out, as he sucked the cigarette. His spectacles were perched on the tip of his nose.

"Yes, I did."

"Oh really? You know what," Jamana said with a voice laden with pain. "It is said that there is no way we can compare our kind with others. It is said that there is no tribe or race to compare ourselves with."

"That is true. And people should not blame me then Jamana."

Jamana fell silent for a while. Then he looked at Jay. "Last time one of the leaders said that if you continue associating yourself with Survival International you will end up like El-Negro."

"Who is El-Negro?"

"He is one of our people whose body was displayed in France for public amusement many years ago."

"Ah, let's forget about the past. We want our own history now."

Jamana nodded and looked away.

Jay looked at him. "That is another way of trying to divert our attention from the real problem."

They were passing several signs encouraging travellers to visit CKGR. They turned to the right and followed another path with the sign post: Welcome to New Xade.

"The inside chick may die, but the outside one will find out how to survive," said Jay getting out of the van and walking towards the huts of his wives.

Jamana indicated with his hand that he still wanted to talk. "You forgot to tell me if you told the reporters that you have changed your mind. Remember what you said after the meeting at Cresta Lodge. I mean that you said that you support the relocation." But Jay walked away waving his hand. Jamana licked his lips, got behind the wheel and left.

# Chapter Thirteen

Greetings from a friend are like medicine. So why not embrace this new friend? Jay was used to receiving letters. But this one! He did not know whether he should take it seriously or not. After his children had read it out to him, he threw it away, annoyed. People like to play with important things, he thought. Then suddenly, unexpectedly, the letter tickled a memory. It was memory of when he had heard Botswana's history from Jamana. Were the British not the ones who had protected Botswana from the South African Boers in the 1800s? Indeed, the British were the people who knew how to solve land disputes. Had they also not helped the country achieve independence in 1966? Perhaps they had forgotten to include the Basarwa when they brought independence.

He ought not to dismiss the letter from the British land "where the sun was said to never set."

Let organizations come and help me and my people go back to CKGR, he thought to himself. He coughed to remove something in his throat. It was regret, this thing in his throat.

If only he could have asked his children about the letter, its contents, details. He would have taken it back to his suitcase and kept it safe among the work permits from the South African mines which were still tucked safely away in the briefcase up to this day.

But then he became preoccupied with Lillian and Drum's promises about how they would help him go back to CKGR. If only the promises would bear fruit. This promise filled his heart, his mind, such that he felt ashamed of being confused by a letter which was only intended to ruin his plans. Particularly when he was on the verge of success. He rubbed his eyes as the longing for Lillian and Drum brought a mixture of bitterness and excitement. But unexpectedly, he nearly burst out laughing. Then he remembered that he was not alone. Present were his children and two wives. His two children had just brought the letter. He tilted back on the chair and the letter on the table close to his right hand fell. He seemed oblivious of it, deeply in thought. Then, his senior wife, Xwaashe, emerged from the other hut.

She entered the loo at the back of the hut. Through the ajar door, she saw him smile and tried to smile back at him.

"Are you well?" she asked, without stopping to hear his response. Jay did not stir and kept silent. Xwaashe stopped at the entrance and supported herself by placing her hands on the door post with one leg suspended in mid step. Still dazed, Jay walked out of the hut. By now Xhwaashe had entered the loo and shut the door.

She also had not noticed the wrinkles on his skin. Jay walked in circles, head held high, both hands in the pocket as if communicating with the sky, or the gods. He walked like a man unsure of the course of action.

As he dropped his head, he seemed to notice the new dew that had fallen on the sandy soil. He went back into the hut, noticed the letter again. He reluctantly picked it up and placed it on the table.

"I was asking if you are well," Xhwaashe asked again as Jay placed the letter on the table. Her eyes also went to the letter. She then moved her eyes away from the letter as she noticed a forlorn look in her husband's face. Xhwaashe went back to weaving a basket.

Three days earlier a man from South Africa had shown interest in her basket and some artefacts during the Kuru Festival, a cultural show where the Basarwa congregate and exhibit their dancing talent. He had promised to come and collect others items and sell them for her in Cape Town. The man had urged her to work on more baskets and other artefacts. But she was suspicious because only a month earlier a Mosarwa woman lost her copyrights to a South African company and was fortunately helped by a certain individual. Xhwaashe had also been confused when the meaning of copyrights was explained to her. But all the same she kept on weaving the basket. Jay had warned her to stop. The previous day their conversation about the baskets nearly degenerated into a quarrel. Perhaps that was what was bothering her husband now, she thought.

At Xhwaashe's question about his well-being, Jay saw the images as he usually did when thinking about the ancestral land, the CKGR; images of his people, not the short smiling woman before him.

Their eyes appeared sad, terrified, almost in chaos. He was choked; depressed that he would never retain the land, never go back to the CKGR. As Jay sat on the chair, he thought: did he leave his job at the South African mines for nothing? Did he learn about the struggle for freedom from South African mines for nothing?

What was that song that the miners used to sing? *Shosholoza*, the struggle song.

Oh those were the days. He buried his head in his hand, Xhwaashe approached him, and a twang of guilt came over her. She unfolded his lifeless arms. And her husband did not even resist. Jay looked up at Xhwaashe.

As they looked deep into each other's eyes, Jay remembered that he had not responded to her question.

"I didn't hear what you said."

"You could have said you heard me but did not understand."

Xhwaashe felt Jay's creased face with her hardened palms. Ever since she had started weaving the threads from the palm tree, her hands were no longer soft. Without a word, Jay stood up and went to his bed. Xhwaashe, with a mixture of disappointment and anxiety on her face, went out to join Motse, the younger wife.

As she emerged from the small hut at the far end of the compound littered with bundles of reeds and some other tools for weaving, Motse saw two strangers emerge from a double cab, a Toyota Hilux. Surprised and curious, she stopped.

The two strangers, a man and a woman, approached her, both smiling at the same time as if their blood flowed together. She knew that they had come for Jay. Their husband had brought trouble.

Motse's heart sank, remembering the good days before the CKGR relocation took place. Oh, those were the days.

"Good day Mma, could we please see Jay," the lady said after a handshake. Motse thought she would speak Afrikaans as some Batswana women married to whites in the Ghanzi area spoke the language fluently. But this one spoke Setswana and even her tone did not suggest that she was from around Kalahari. From the man, Motse sensed the accent of a person from D'kar, in Kalahari. He also spoke unrefined, mild Setswana as indeed most whites around Kalahari do. She dropped her bundles with care and left the new visitors with Xhwaashe who had just joined them and confirmed that Jay was in. Motse went away to call her husband, with her thoughts racing in different directions. What could the purpose of these visitors be? What crime had Jay committed? Hardly a week ago had they not been visited by some security agents? They had warned Jay to stop urging people to go back to CKGR. But these ones did not look like security agents. Something important might have happened in the capital city, Gaborone. Motse knocked. There was no reply. She pushed the door and entered. Jay raised his sleepy eyes from the pillow.

"What is it?" His head fell back on the pillow. He showed no surprise when he was told there were people outside looking for him. He expected anything, anyone and everything.

But who could these visitors be? Jay wondered after Motse had told him about the two strangers.

"Did you say a man and a woman?" he asked, unable to hide his curiosity. To Xhwaashe and Motse's surprise, Jay's face lit up upon meeting the two strangers. Even the strangers called him by name. The two wives were relieved as they exchanged meaningful glances. They left Jay and his two visitors. The third wife, Mmabatho, had gone to Ghanzi.

"Come in." Jay led the way inside the hut as the two visitors looked at his hut both with admiration and scorn. They sat at a table.

"I can only remember your name Mr. Drum." Jay sat close to the wooden bookshelf facing his two visitors.

"Lillian is the name," said the lady in the manner of a white woman. Jay thought he had picked up the lifestyle of Botswana's middle class, those who went to expensive English medium schools that were now a business in the country.

A smile which confused and trapped him, spread over Lillian's face confirming his belief that the lady must be one of the daughters of a rich man, perhaps a politician. Jay kept glancing at her but failing to maintain eye contact with her as she spoke. He noticed that she was light skinned and had soft hair which she kept pushing gently away, the way a white woman would do. Her teeth were white, except the gold tooth which Jay seemed to notice for the first time. She stretched her red skirt to cover her knees and this act made Jay uncomfortable. She wore glasses through which her large relaxed eyes could be seen clearly, except when they caught reflections from the images on Jay's wall, an eland and decorations.

A small handbag hung over her shoulders and was slung across her well-shaped breasts. She smiled as Jay dropped his head before looking at Drum who cleared his throat, a sign that he wanted to speak. But the man said nothing or he had nothing to say. Lillian's eyes were relaxed; she was beautiful, a woman who could bring excitement to a man's boring life. But at that moment, Jay thought he heard his father's voice warning him that a man who marries for beauty only brings trouble to himself. Thus he contented himself with his three wives. Her smile was convincing. She seemed to see through him, penetrating his brown animal skin jacket and into his head. She is not my type, something inside Jay said, as he avoided her eyes.

"Can I make you some coffee?" Jay panicked as he stood up, holding his hands behind him, like a servant waiting for orders from his masters.

"We have just had some," Drum said as he looked at Lillian as if to get assurance that he also spoke on her behalf. He then shifted his eyes from Lillian to Jay's cultural artefacts which seemed to have arrested his attention.

"Yes, we are okay." It was Lillian as she tore her eyes away from the little pictures on the wall. She then stole quick glances at her hand bag as if it was something that needed her attention, a baby.

"We have to assist you my brother, Jay," she said. Lillian smiled again as Jay returned from the smouldering fire where he had wanted to prepare coffee. He nodded, almost trustingly, pushing some papers on the table in discomfort.

"We thought we had to hasten our help," Drum said hurriedly as if to drive away the discomfort he had sensed in Jay. His eyes followed the papers that Jay had pushed. A letter with a British stamp caught his attention.

"People really want to go back to the CKGR," Drum added, his eyes still surveying the letter. He tried to hide his curiosity but his mouth watered for the letter's contents as he swallowed a lump in his throat.

"How are you going to help me find my people and make them visible in the eyes of the leaders?" Somehow Jay was still confused. How had the Basarwa's rights become so important to such people? Had their type not kept his kind at the cattle posts?

As he always did in such moments, he remembered an incident in which two Basarwa were nearly hanged after they killed their master. The pair was angry after their master lashed them for allegedly slaughtering his cow near Serowe village.

"Our organization," Lillian broke into Jay's thoughts as she fumbled for something from her bag.

"As we said at our last meeting, my organization called Ditshwanelo exists to help people who find themselves at the receiving end like you."

A pen in one hand and a file in the other, Lillian explained how her organization worked.

Drum was still struggling to join in the conversation as his eyes were still glued to the letter with a British stamp.

The organization had helped, or rather fought against the hanging of individuals in Botswana, arguing that the act was inhuman. Jay knew that if someone killed another he would be hanged and he nearly asked Lillian if they had succeeded.

But he was powerless in the presence of his visitors, his protectors. Then he remembered the two Basarwa men.

Gays also had rights, as that was their sexual orientation. Abortion or denying the baby the right to life was also not welcome by Ditshwanelo. Jay lost cohesion in this explanation. Some of the things he could not understand and things like gays he had never heard of before.

"So we are here to help you too," Lillian met Jay's confused face. Jay dropped his eyes, failing to face her striking features. He noticed that today she had applied what he later learnt was makeup.

"That is true," Drum declared with a warm, convincing voice.

Though a daughter of the soil, Lillian had studied in South Africa, the land of Mandela who had defeated apartheid. There was nothing that could stand in her way. She had also studied in England, the land of the mighty Queen whose hand had touched every part of the earth. Mma Mosadinyana- the lovely queen. Was she not the one who ensured that Botswana got independence? So armed with knowledge from Mandela's and the Queen's lands, what could stand before Lillian? Nothing was impossible. She knew how things worked and, as she explained to Jay, who cupped his chin in his hands, she was one of the students who had fought apartheid.

"You remember the Soweto students' uprising?" she asked after Jay told her that he left his job at the South African mines to come and free his people. Lillian's eyes seemed to be searching his thoughts. Jay nodded and Lillian, urged on, explained that she had chosen to study in South Africa to learn about human injustice. She had wanted to help her brothers and sisters in South Africa. That dream was achieved in 1994 when South Africa became a democratic country under the leadership of Mandela. Though she was not instrumental in shaping the democracy, she had learnt that human rights were as important as human life itself. That became a vision; she became a Human Rights activist. Lillian later walked in that vision when she set up Ditshwanelo - an organization ensuring that human rights are not trampled upon. To understand how human rights work, Lillian explained, one should have studied subjects or pursued disciplines like law, so Lillian reached for a file from her handbag to show him her credentials and possibly convince him that she was true to the Basarwa's cause.

Jay raised his head and pulled at his trousers, fighting his shame. He struggled to force a smile, but only bit his lower lips. As he began to speak, Lillian stopped him with her enchanting smile.

"You do not look like... you know." Lillian failed to find the right words to use.

She leaned back on the chair to survey the bookshelves close to Jay. Jay nodded as he too looked at the books. He understood. Her words were clear in that look, the look she gave him, his books, everything about him. Rumours that she had heard about Jay. His ability to engage leaders in tough debates, the way he was respected, his appearance, his hut, his car, his children.

These were the missing words. After all these years there were now educated Basarwa, though not many. Some had recently added their voice to the CKGR issue in the media. Perhaps Lillian thought Jay was one of them. Indeed there had been some press releases from their organization, the FPK, led by Jay himself. Jay looked at her but his gaze did not linger much as Lillian simultaneously raised her head slowly from the book shelves and the picture of Jay and others at a beach in America.

She then remembered reading somewhere in the newspapers that Jay had been to America to see that country's President, appealing to him to assist the Basarwa. Why did he have to bypass us, she thought. At least we are here now, Lillian said quietly to herself. Jay swallowed a lump in his throat, which quickly grew into an outbreak of sweat, rivulets streaming down his body.

"We will have to tell the authorities that what they are doing is not in your people's interest." Drum stood up and yawned before he could continue. Lillian made as if she would rise to her feet but only leaned against the chair. Again it was as though another thought trailed at the back of many that she had already shared with Jay as spoken words. Drum's eyes wandered to the alluring letter again. He squeezed his eyes and made an inaudible sound in his throat. A regret. He could and should have brought his glasses along. This time as if by sheer coincidence, the letter caught Lillian's attention. But she was too preoccupied with her assistance to Jay and his people. She managed to rise to her feet.

"Leave everything to us," she said before she added hurriedly. "Rather, we will speed up the process of Going back to CKGR. That is Old Xade isn't it." Jay said yes, as he walked behind his visitors as they went out. At that moment he saw the letter too. Should he show them the letter? Would they not say that he was foolish to believe in such childish letters? He did not want Lillian and Drum losing confidence in him. Where would he get help? Though he was still awaiting response from the US president and other European countries' head of states, one had to ask assistance from the people within proximity.

Back on the hut, Jay peered at the letter again and his head buzzed. Without warning, he dozed off still thinking how he should react to the British Prince's letter.

# Chapter Fourteen

It attracted people from different parts of the world; Parliamentarians from Denmark, the European Union and Norway sent their representatives to investigate. But that was not all. The CKGR was also discussed in Britain's House of Lords, their Parliament, just as they had done with the marriage of the first President of the country, Sir Seretse Khama. This was because they knew better.

Were they not the ones who had created the reserve? So they could not be left out because they were worried about what they had done, their intentions.

But that was not the greatest thing. Hirschfield, a leader of the Basarwa, had met with the Prince of Britain himself before he died. That was in London.

The Prince of the great Queen of Britain, Mma Mosadinyana, as Batswana fondly called her, was heard to have supported the CKGR. He found himself at one with CKGR. He could not, did not sleep but only thought about the Kalahari, the CKGR before and after his visit there. This was an African adventure, his CKGR ambition.

It was a rich culture that he had never seen, especially the trance dance. People from all over the world should come and witness how spiritual people here in the desert could be. The trance dance, it is said, still replays in the Prince's mind even up to this day. Sometimes people said he visited the CKGR to watch the dance without people or even reporters knowing.

0-0-0-0-0

The trance dance...It replayed many times in the Prince's mind. And he remembered it as if it were yesterday as he now sat in his library in London, thinking of how he would help Jay and his people. The events at the CKGR seven years earlier unfolded in his mind.

The sky was cloudless. Only the orange of the fire illuminated the dark, making it look sacred. The illuminated dark appeared spiritual for the occasion. The fire light deepened the darkness around the place.

Women clad in animal skin skirts clapped their hands, their breasts curved upward, though most of them were elderly. They wore decorated ostrich egg shells which shone like diamonds when they reflected light from the fire. They sang and at the same time bowed their heads, in measured steps, raising them in time to the four male spiritual leaders who raised their feet and stepped the ground with such dignity that it shook with delight. It was as if their lives depended on it, the soil covered with bed grass. When the fire lit the women's faces they appeared sacred too. They wore pieces of skins that covered their breasts. The men were bare from the chest to the waists and wore loincloths which passed between their buttocks. In their right hands were zebras' whisks made from the end of the horses' tails. In their left hands were digging sticks which they used for support as they limped with measured steps. Their ankles wore a decoration of rattles which added a rhythm to the women's songs. Whenever they stepped their feet on the ground, the rattles would echo throughout the night. The rattles rose powerfully against the women's voices.

In a state of unconsciousness, the four men touched the women on their heads. Their faces wore beads of perspiration. Suddenly, three of them turned into hunters and the other turned into prey. The three men poisoned the tips of their arrows and the wild animal became alert, sensing the presence of the three hunters.

Meanwhile, the women had changed their songs into those of death. One of the hunters aimed and shot at once. The wild animal was shot on the leg but managed to run away. The three hunters still circling the women followed it. At last, the wild animal, exhausted, fell to the ground. Suddenly, the wounded animal rose to its feet and rushed forward. The three hunters in pursuit halted and bowed their heads to the ground as if detecting something or as if waiting for a voice to tell them what to do next. They stamped their feet heavier than before, and stamped together in unison as if they had rehearsed this. They made as if they would stumble on each other but they did not. The wild animal fell to the ground again and the three hunters stamped the ground heavier than before.

Now the knocking together of their rattles was loud enough to be heard over the women singing. The dance was now done with measured steps and their breathing came in gasps, making the ground's surface quiver. The women were like drums to the dancing of the men as they danced in harmony with their songs. Again the man who acted as a wild animal jumped forward and began to look around as if he would recognize some people from the darkness. The three others who acted as hunters began to follow him closely. At the same time one of them would raise one of his thighs and the others took turns placing their heads between his raised thigh as if to smell something there. The women worked themselves into a frenzy when they saw this.

Suddenly, their singing broke off the moment the man who had been acting as a wild animal fell to the ground for the third time. The three who had been acting as hunters abandoned sniffing each other, rushed to the wild animal and fell on top of it. The men began to groan. It was then that spectators noticed that on their left wrists the men wore elands' leather amulets. The men's fingers closed around the beds of grass on their sides and they grasped it as if in pain.

The sacred songs and the presence of the spirits seemed to leave the place the moment the men fell to the ground and the women broke off and stopped singing. They broke out of the circle and came to hover over the exhausted men as if they feared they had died. There was a constant clatter from the ostrich necklaces as the women moved their heads up and down over the men lying down on the ground.

The fire seemed to die down as well. The ground which the four men had stamped so heavily was now trodden into dust. The bed of grass that had been there was soiled. Then the women rose and the four men arose quickly appearing as fresh as ever. They walked as if they had springs in their torsos, seeming to have regained their youth.

The Prince had sat on top of a safari van, enjoying the best view. The dance had been sacred as those present felt the presence of the ancestral spirits. The trance dance was terrifying and exciting to watch, the Prince reflected later. Some of the tourists had chosen to stand with the crowd to see this spiritual dance. They were not disappointed by what they had read in books, tourism magazines and in the newspapers like The New York Times and The UK Guardian. There was something about this culture that made it very appealing. One had to see the Basarwa in action during the trance dance to appreciate how spiritual and religious they were.

0-0-0-0-0

The Prince was suddenly jolted out of his reverie when a book fell from his lap. As he sat now in his spacious library, he pulled out a book, entitled "History of Botswana." He opened a chapter on page 45 and began to read the passage he was interested in.

"The Central Kalahari Game Reserve was set up in 1961 by the British government. That was shortly before independence in 1966."

The Prince put the book away abruptly and did not want to look at it again. He then recalled his conversation with a South African man. In fact, the Prince had told people in Britain about his experience.

"I was thrilled," he had said. "Those people have the

most interesting skills and survival strategies I have never seen or read about in the books. They must not be wished away like that. I can't just watch them being ill-treated like that if they do not want to."

That was in 1987. He had taken a trip to CKGR to see for himself, as the people would say. He loved the way the Basarwa were friendly, the way they were close to each, the way they loved each other.

The Prince also recalled his first encounter with the hunters and gatherers. They had gone out the following day after he had watched the trance dance. He was accompanied by Hirschfield and his friends. Hirschfield was explaining something and emphasizing it with his arrows while his other hand rested on his bow slung across his shoulder.

"Plants are used as herbs to heal the sick," Hirschfield explained after the dance as the Prince gazed at him with revived interest. This was after he had watched Hirschfield rub sticks together to make the fire that was later used for the trance dance. That was also when he had asked some of the healers if they had ever attempted to cure HIV/AIDS. They had just looked at him with wonder. "What disease was that?" some had asked. To them the disease was a stranger, a new thing.

Then he understood that indeed the CKGR was a place detached from the problems besieging the scientific world. This was an ancient world. And day and night, his interest in this ancient world overwhelmed him.

"I would like to learn how you build snares," the Prince had said as he moved from the van to where the fire was beginning to build up. Three men had gathered around the fire as sunset approached. The Prince stared at their mouths as they spoke among themselves, bemused. Out of curiosity and wonder he had asked to learn their click languages too. He tried to suck the tongue behind the teeth, but only succeed in biting his tongue.

How peaceful these people were, he reflected later. Even

historians never documented any tribal wars among them, he remembered from the Botswana or African history books he had read. The Basarwa women peered at him, bemused as well, their legs folded before them and their heads supported by their hands. Some had their heads bowed. The Prince later set out with Hirschfield and his men as they wanted to take him out for a hunting session. Apart from the bows and arrows, Hirschfield and his men had pouches made from springbok and eland fur.

"We have been doing this before the white men came," Hirschfield explained about his people's hunting and gathering lifestyle.

"Even before the black man came," added another man.

Hirschfield paused as he took an enormous pull from some leaves of tobacco which one of his friends had rolled using a newspaper. Each of the men had a turn to smoke as they stood near the Okwa valley in the CKGR. Hirschfield had to destroy the tobacco as they approached a group of springboks. One of the men raised some dust in the air to gauge the direction of the wind. He then indicated with his hand that they should go towards the south.

"This is to avoid the animals sensing our presence." Hirschfield explained to the Prince. Two of the springboks raced after each other, leaping and keeping their legs in the air before landing their small hoofs on the ground. It was a spectacle to behold. Some were still grazing with their heads bowed. Hirschfield pulled the Prince by the hand and the men dropped flat on the ground. However, the Prince was left standing as he became fascinated by a scar on Hirschfield's left eye. He recalled that Hirschfield had explained, as he usually did, with his hands raised in the air, that he had survived a lion attack. There was also an incision between his eyes and other similar cuts on the cheeks. The razor had left scars which looked like Roman numerals, the Prince observed.

"The hair between the eyes of an eland had been removed

and inserted into these incisions." Hirschfield had explained at the Prince's curiosity.

"Is that why you can even survive a lion's attack?" the Prince had asked, bemused again.

"Yes," agreed Hirschfield. "This is meant to instill the power of the spiritual eland in me."

The Prince had nodded and the other man continued explaining.

"The eland represents the most potent animal in our society," Hirschfield continued. "We respect it and we believe that it is close to our gods. It has immense spiritual power, more than anything. That spiritual power is present in the fat of the male one. We did not choose it. It was chosen by our god. It also unites and protects us from harm. In that fat lie supernatural powers."

By then the Prince was half-listening, thinking or remembering that he had read in one of the books where the Shamans were said to transform into wild animals.

"We believe that some animals have certain powers which we use to heal and make rain," Hirschfield had brought the Prince out of his day dream.

"That is also part of our dance and we feature that in our songs and the dance that you have just witnessed." By then the men were crawling and were within striking range. On the flat sands they crawled on their stomachs. But before the Prince could see the spectacle unfold in its entirety, a lorry came and frightened the intended targets before the Basarwa men could shoot.

Thinking of the trance dance now, the extraordinary hunting and gathering lifestyle that had brought wonder, the Prince felt pain surging upward. He could not understand it. He had travelled across Britain hoping to hear someone talking about how they could help. He wanted to be told about the relocation from the CKGR, but there was no one.

"There is a genuine problem," he muttered to himself, as though addressing the absent Basarwa.

At that moment, the Prince opened a magazine and recognized the man the authorities were talking about. Was this the same man whom he had been with in the CKGR with Hirschfield when they had gone hunting after the trance dance? Was this the same man who had been in Britain?

So the man was now a leader of the organization that Hirschfield had formed, FPK.

0-0-0-0-0

And the memories of the Prince's visit to the CKGR were revived again. It was a hot long drive to the CKGR from Gaborone. Even at the big gate of the game reserve, signs showed that they still had a long way to go. Kori campsites -2 km, Letlhahau - 41 km, Piper Pan - 100 km, Xade -170 km, Xaka - 240 km.

He had been at Molapo settlement where he had shared watermelon with the residents. Jay was the same man who had sat atop a wooden stool. In his right hand was a wooden knife which he used to slice the watermelon. To his right were his two wives while on his left were his children. The watermelon was shared amongst them. Jay would slice the watermelon carefully before raising his head to talk. Discarded slices lay beside him, his wives and children with one lying before the Prince. Pips were collected for future cultivation.

That was before the Prince had enjoyed his nights in Gaborone, the capital where there were neon lights, not much different from what was classified as towns in Britain. The names in Gaborone also made the Prince feel that he was in Africa.

Haile Selasie, Nelson Mandela Drive, Samora Machel Drive, Sam Nujoma Drive.

He had also landed at Sir Seretse Khama International Airport. However, there were also things that reminded him of England, like the banks, Barclays Bank.

Apart from the heat, he felt as though he was home.

Suddenly, as he sat now with the book and the pen on his table in his lavish library, the voices of the CKGR residents, some of whom the Prince had not seen, challenged him to come out and support the people opposing the relocation. The voices advised him to act in harmony with the Basarwa. He would not fail the Basarwa, his ancestors' subjects. He had to tell the world how and why the British created the CKGR. He took out another notebook and pen having quickly forgotten that there was already another book and a pen in front of him.

But the urgency to write was disturbed by his shaking hands. What was wrong with these hands?

He had already resolved that the relocation should wait for him to explain. As he was about to make a phone call to tell Jay that he would not help, the damage had already been done. His steward brought the Monday newspaper early that morning. There was a smile on the steward's face, excitement. The headlines.

And upon on seeing them, the Prince who was about to rise to his feet, slumped back in his chair. All the headlines said the same thing. Reporters? Where did they get the news? But had he momentarily forgotten that there was a Press conference when he had met the Basarwa? How soon he forgot.

"Prince Battles for the Basarwa." Those were the headlines. And when he peered at the paper closely, staring at him was none other than Jay on the front page. The Prince nodded. Now he would not fail. He had to. He wrote a letter to Jay and the Basarwa.

# Chapter Fifteen

The honey badger smells a honey comb. The authorities now suspected everyone, especially when they read in the newspapers that even some members of the royal family in Britain wanted to help in taking the Basarwa back to the CKGR. Who was Jay?

Where was he from? How could we tell that he looked like this or that?

"As I said, you should identify yourself," said the Minister of Local Government at a meeting in the new settlement, New Xade. The meeting was aimed at convincing residents to forget about going back to CKGR and that what Jay and Survival International as well as the Prince had said in the media were mere dreams, in fact bad dreams.

"Your name, the organization or village you represent."

Jay was silent for a time as if he was not sure of his answer to the Minister. But his eyes were on the Minister forcing her to drop her eyes like a girl being proposed to by an elderly man whom she should be calling father.

At that moment it seemed the question that was on each guest was what nationality was Jay?

"We have told police and immigration officials to tighten the screws," said the Minister silently as her lips parted. At last she could not contain her thoughts. She spoke up. "I would like to assure you that we have closed all the loopholes in our laws," she said to the silent residents of the CKGR in the new settlements.

"In fact, if the man is in this country as alleged by our unpatriotic newspapers, we will have no choice but to deport him right away. Like many others. We are going to talk plainly because myself and others know that you people of

CKGR are not capable of doing that. You can't even hurt a newly born hare. Pour out all your troubles. After all you know, or let me remind you that the government is like a chief or a leader. You know our saying that a chief is like a rubbish heap: all rubbish is heaped on it. We have to protect our country and rid it of extremists, mad people. Or else we will have a country like Somalia or Israel though being a country which Jesus had blessed."

"We have to fight, because now there is a certain man and some international organizations who have touched us where it hurts. Can you believe it when they lie about our diamonds, our modern cattle, where will we be without them? They say you are being relocated because of diamonds and that you are ill-treated because unlike diamonds, you are not shining. I know that you people of CKGR cannot labour such stupid ideas." The Minister spoke as if she did not want to mention the names of the person and organization she spoke of.

Suddenly a voice said, "We are going back home." The Minister paused, taken aback. She waited for the voice to repeat itself, but it seemed to have died as quickly as it had come.

"Residents, we have heard your concerns," continued the Minister. "We know that there is no one here who can teach you how to hunt."

"Or herd cattle at the cattle post," added another guest.

The Minister laughed and continued to tell the residents that they were looking for Jay, not a man from the cattle post. The Minister continued explaining to the obedient residents.

"We don't want a man from the CKGR. We want a man who has penned articles in the media," she explained. She added that they did not travel all the way from Gaborone to come and listen to anyone who only knew about how to use bows and arrows. Or someone who could tell how big or small a wild animal was by merely looking at its droppings.

"Let me tell you that we have come here from government departments," she said with the air of knowledge which she tried best to impart to the residents.

"As the most sympathetic country in the world, we have a mobile government to ensure that there is justice, water, housing, resources, development, money, agriculture and so on. We reach out to every citizen so that they do not say the country is Gaborone only. For instance, there are ministers, permanent secretaries, police officers, court clerks, district commissioners; every government department you can think of, you shall find it here, represented." She paused for her words to strike her listeners.

"So, you can see that we did not migrate with the government from Gaborone to come and waste resources and our energy here for nothing or waste time with hunters. What can we benefit from hunting lessons? We want the man who is a real stumbling block to the relocation. Not a man who wears eland horns and animal skin jackets. This is not a time for poachers; the police and wildlife officials will take care of that, will deal with that." She paused and took a bottle of mineral water, much to the chagrin of thirsty residents who could only lick their lips with saliva, thinking about the water supply cut at CKGR. She took the sip slowly and the liquid oozed down her throat like running water.

"We want intellectuals," she said. "People whose heads are full of education. Those who when you cut them with a knife they bleed education, not blood from wildlife animals. If you want licenses for hunting you can go and see wildlife officials, or if you want a job to herd cattle. Please do that later. I'm sure some of our guests need herd boys. Or check the Daily News and apply. This is not the right forum. We want Jay. If you recall, we have just sent a professor packing. Professor Cain Bad from Australia. You remember that lecture at the University of Botswana. He wanted to plant the seed of disunity in the country. We do not want such elements. Even the courts agreed with us that such a man was a danger to the security of the country. He cried to the judges when they told him that they had done justice to him. What was he crying for since he has his own country. But we know that those were crocodile tears. He is jealous." It was a harsh dry cough like the Kalahari Desert sand cracking during summer that made the Minister pause. The man who had spoken of Going Back to CKGR stood up. His hands were in his pockets.

Then he suddenly removed one of his hands from his pocket. They glanced at him in confusion. The security agents watched the man carefully. Their eyes never left his hand as it came out of the pocket. They sighed relief when they realized what he had taken out. Some even smiled. It was a cigarette. The man's cheeks were hollow as if the CKGR issue had sucked too much flesh from his body. He took a few puffs and watched the smoke curl as if it was an exciting thing to do, a game that he was fond of playing. He laughed as if the meeting or the words that had been spoken meant nothing to him. A voice said, heap all the accusations and blame the Minister. But another told him to wait. Still with the cigarette in his hand, he moved away. People created space for him. But he did not go far. He stood there and started smoking. This gave the Station Commander of Ghazi police station a chance to approach the Minister and her delegates. He whispered something in their ears. After the man was done with smoking, he came back to the place where he had stood before. People created space for him again.

"Could you please help me find my people and make them visible to the eyes like a shining diamond?" the man said turning his eyes from the officials to the people. His gestures were as if he would leave New Xade settlement at once and go back to the CKGR in that instant. In those gestures, it was clear that there were words that he could not wait to deliver.

"We are not here to be asked questions," said the Minster "but to explain to the people so that they can see the advantages of the relocation. We do not know of lost people."

"But you said that in this country there should be dialogue," said the man raising his eyes.

"At least say who you are," the Minister said, almost losing her patience. "Then we will take it from there."

"For your own information and broadcasting," the man said, "I'm the Jay you spoke of." Still Jay did not lower his eyes out of respect for a top government official like the Minister. Jay's introduction caused a big stir among the guests. The residents were on the other hand, it seemed full of happiness.

The important guests swayed on their seats. There was a cough there and there. The majority of people narrowed their eyes. So this was the man feared by the authorities.

"When you came here you said you were looking for Jay, isn't it?"

By now everyone, residents, the minister and representatives from various departments had turned their eyes on Jay. Some surveyed him, holding their chins in their cupped hands, in utter disbelief. So this was Jay, they seemed to be saying.

"I said it before and I know the police and wildlife officials can testify."

"This is not a court of law," the Minister said, still unable to hide or contain her curiosity and doubt. "You said you are Jay from where?"

The people looked on with a mixture of pity and fear at the man they knew so well. Admiration was written in their faces. But the guests had contempt. There was no need to be afraid of the man they called Jay now. Despite the background stories that had been written in the newspapers and the articles about the court case, Jay was invisible in the eyes of the Minister. Those unpatriotic newspapers had exaggerated the truth. The Minister put on her spectacles to help her eyes. She saw nothing there that could frighten her or anything that demanded respect, or commanded dignity. But, only for a moment.

"I'm Jay from the Kalahari Desert," he said with a steady voice, "or what you call Central Kalahari Game Reserve (CKGR)."

"Oh that is you," the Minister said with something like a mixture of a false smile and shock on her face. She looked about in shame. A big weight was beginning to be taken off from her and her colleagues as they sighed hard too.

The Minster shrugged, wondering if a spokesperson of the Basarwa could just look like them; thin eyes, tan skin, stunted hair and all the features that were associated with Jay's people. After realizing that Jay belonged to the lowest of the low, she started to speak with the voice of a strict parent scolding an unrepentant and ungrateful child.

"Mr. Jay, I have just asked Ditshwanelo if you are to represent the Basarwa but they told me that they would speak on behalf of the Basarwa."

"I'm what?"

"You are not the right person to represent the voices of the Basarwa. We would rather find someone ourselves, and not from the Basarwa. You can't do it because you are part of them. You are part of the problem, so to speak. You have nothing, you know nothing."

"But it has happened before," Jay said loudly as if addressing the whole country.

"Didn't blacks used to cry that the whites refused to hear their voices or allow them to compete for top jobs?" The Minister was more shocked now. Was it true that Jay was from CKGR? Where did he learn to speak? Where did he get the voice?

And indeed Jay had wanted, had in fact, roped in Ditshwanelo for further negotiations, as the Minister suggested. After all, Ditshwanelo had helped two Basarwa men escape the death penalty. It is said that even when the Judge had pronounced Section 203 which dealt with the death penalty, the two men had remained indifferent as if they were not involved in the case. Or as if to them, the death penalty meant nothing. Even the booming voice of the judge as he read out the judgment. "You, Thaloganyo Makole and Dira Gadibonwe are to be hanged by the neck until you die." It had seemed like a voice from outside their normal life, a foreign voice, something that had no consequence on their lives. It is said that the two death row inmates even chuckled when the judge asked if they understood.

The men were convicted of murder after they killed the owner of an ox that they had allegedly stolen. The man had pounced on them while they were watching over the meat to dry. Ditshwanelo had then managed to get the death sentence reversed. This Jay knew so well and he had thought Ditshwanelo would be a partner in fighting for the cause of his people. Despite his relationship with Survival International and the case before the court he had not ruled out Ditshwanelo as a partner in the struggle for his people. But now the arrogance of the Minister, her naked pride, reminded him where he belonged in the society: the lowest of the low.

It pricked him like a needle sliding into the skin of a newly born baby. And Jay always breathed hard when he was angry. Perhaps he would never seek help from anyone. Seeking help always reminded some arrogant people that they were doing his people a favour. He could survive without them. He would launch the fight to go back home alone and find his people alone. His eyes blinked rapidly.

His nose was aching. In fact he was struck by a headache. And like any illness, it needed a cure - Going back to CKGR.

"You and your kind must leave us alone."

"Mr Jay, please," said the District Commissioner for Ghanzi, the area under which CKGR fell. He made a request, an appeal, the way a father would appeal to his son who thought he was now a man who could make decisions on his own.

"Let's ask questions," said the District Commissioner in a voice that carried traces of pain, "not forgetting that we are addressing elders."

"Leave my people alone," Jay said throwing his hands in the air, "and take with you all the developments and civilizations that you have." He continued speaking, showing no indication that he had got the message or advise from the Distinct Commissioner.

He turned his eyes from the security agents to the delegates. "Let me warn you that I'm as educated as you are." He paused and then continued. "My people were here before the British colonized this country. So you can see that we are older than this country. We never invited them. They were invited by your grandfathers, or the three chiefs. But they never troubled us, I mean the British and those three chiefs. The first President also did not trouble us. Today we are asking ourselves questions with no answers, because you are failing to answer those questions. Anyway, let me share with you the question that has been troubling me and my people before I sit down. Why are you making trouble for us? Lastly, if you do not do as I say, I'm going to reveal the shocking truth about the relocation."

But the authorities, it seemed, made light of Jay's statement, perhaps because they knew better.

Later the story that Jay was opposing relocation and making strange demands, was spread throughout the country by newspapers. Many people laughed with contempt when they heard this. It was news. This was because they were still shocked; never before had such a thing happened. People were still shocked that a man from the lowest of the low and from people only known for hunting and gathering and being cattle herders of wealthy Batswana could do that. But had the guests not narrowed their eyes in shock that day? The former residents of the CKGR were touched by

Jay's voice, but in the presence of the guests they concealed their emotions.

As the meeting progressed, there was change in the way the Minister addressed Jay. She learnt that he was not from the university like that deported professor but was from the CKGR. Shame and disappointment were clear on her face. This man would be taken care of very easily, her gestures seemed to suggest. The wildlife officials and the police will take care of the situation. It did not even require the District Commissioner, she reflected as she struggled to fight shame. It was a small matter given the fact that they now knew who Jay was. The guests thought that he must have left somebody's cattle to come and disrupt the meeting.

The Minister sighed.

"Jay, please sit down," she said with something that even a child could not mistake for a false smile on her face. "We have heard your worries," she added. "There is no need to invite the whole world or Survival International, British MPs and even their Prince. We are capable of ruling ourselves. Let me remind you that our independence was gained in 1966. So if since then people here have not seen the benefits of that, we are sorry and we believe that the relocation will help. They are really suffering from thirst and hunger."

"You are right," Jay said. "Since then and now nothing has changed to my people except that the country is now hoisting its flag. Are they not the ones all over the country herding cattle while you watch TVs in Gaborone and hold conferences and cocktail parties everyday?"

Perhaps it was true that Jay should have been herding somebody's cattle just like some of his people. But the CKGR issue had come into his life. It had the effect of crushing the shame associated with his tribe. Again it could not be said that asking questions was unheard of in the society, but never before had they been experienced from the smallest and lowest tribe which many held in contempt.

"Jay, Botswana does not mean Gaborone only," continued the Minister. "There is what we call boundaries. And this reserve is part of the country. What will become of the country if people were to make their own rules? Jay, think about it."

"A man does not move out of his hut," Jay said, "and leave the graveyards of his ancestors like that."

Jay turned his gaze from the guests to his people. Most former residents of the CKGR sat with their hands between their laps.

"You are asking us to confront death," he surveyed the guests again. "And you do not have to worry anymore. I'm not a stranger in your midst. Perhaps some of you had wanted to see me at court. I hardly set my foot there these days. This is so because that is something new to us. I have realized with a terrible pain that the court is something beyond the knowledge of my people. In addition, I might be a stranger because you have always regarded our way of life as strange and held us in contempt. You have even presumed to think for us. But I was not taught that saying no means that one is a stranger. Can you please let us go back home?" As Jay said this, he removed one of his hands from his pocket.

"Were you there when the British declared this a reserve?" asked the Minister after Jay had given her a chance to chip in. "Or which history books have you read and which university…?"

Now Jay and the minister engaged in a form of education, educating each other.

"All the education," Jay cut the Minister short, "that you have received at the universities I got it while in my mother's womb. Diplomas, degrees, you name them. So it is not for those who have been to learning institutions to tell my people what is good for them. It is I who should be telling you how and what to learn from us."

The guests coughed. Where did such a man get the

power to say no? This unexpected advice from Jay made the Minister lose her calm, but she tried to conceal this.

"Jay, please, this is how a government operates," she said bowing her head. "We move our people when the need arises. For instance, we have destroyed people's shacks which they called houses in a location called Mogoditshane and Tsolamosese in the capital city, Gaborone. At times we even give the new locations new names. For instance, the location that people will be relocated to will no longer be called Xade. But because we want your people to migrate with their culture we have not changed the name. It will only be called New Xade. Perhaps we should appoint you a chief."

The Minister remembered the Kamanakao case in which the Bayei tribe had taken the government to court over chieftainship. The court had ruled in favour of the Bayei then. So she did not want the government to suffer such embarrassment again.

"People should be happy seeing such a country such as ours," the Minister continued, "growing up seeing developments springing before our eyes. Just imagine if our colonizers had discovered minerals before they let us hoist our own flag. Perhaps as we speak you have been sent by those who are jealous of our success story."

"I say can you please let my people go home?" Jay said as if the Minister's message had not entered his ears. The way Jay spoke with authority stung the guests. He should not talk as though he was a government representative. Who was he to represent people's thinking?

"Perhaps I should appoint you a paramount chief then, before you start calling yourself Paramount Chief of the Basarwa," said the Minister now with a smile. "But I also wonder what the other paramount chiefs would say." There was a brief break as the government men and women whispered among themselves. The Minister stood up again. She glanced at Jay and then spoke to the residents.

"We hope that the people will not heed what this man had just said," she said, pointing at Jay. "He has already broken the law." She nodded,. "The law of sedition. He was inciting and mobilizing people to take arms against the government, rather use bows and arrows. He has also invaded other people's freedom. He wanted people not to relocate. He has the right to freedom but he should not take away other people's freedom to remain silent and do as their hearts tell them."

Addressing the residents and taking away her eyes from Jay, the Minister said, "I hope you will live happily in the new settlement." She coughed. "With these clinics, schools and government handouts," she continued but now with half her mind on Jay's words. Though she had weighed the trouble that Jay was making, and the way he was being uncooperative, she did not want to take chances with such a man as others had done.

"But the police and wildlife will talk to him and guide him," said the Minister. She added that Jay had a strange character. "We would like to send other officials to come and investigate. Unlike other law abiding citizens who lower their eyes out of respect for the elders this man does not. He did not even greet us." "

Jay stared ahead in silence. Everyone stopped talking. It was as if in his silent temper he was saying meaningless things.

"I said it before," he said in a croaky voice. And as usual, apart from the horns and fur jacket, the Minister realized that there was nothing striking about him and his face appeared to have aged ahead of time. But Jay had this calm, which demanded respect. When he spoke his voice was raised, the way a man would warn his neighbour across the fence that separates their compounds. He put his other hand in his pocket and CKGR residents exchanged meaningful glances. They seemed to grasp the meaning of his words.

"Leave that man alone," said the Minister.

"I know you were willing to relocate, weren't you? You see, you are silent because you agreed to relocate. It is evident that the man who is telling you to go to CKGR is an outsider," the Minister continued.

"He is an outsider. That is why the court said he cannot launch an application on your behalf. Do you see that some of you have been led by a man with questionable sanity? Anyway, we will take him to Lobatse Mental Hospital if he continues saying things that can only make sense to a mad man. This man claims that he can intimidate a government like ours. Even if we are an African government, have been colonized, our silence, our kindness and peace that we are known for the world over should not be used against us by foreign opportunists," she went on.

"We have also realized that the man is not familiar with the way our government takes care of its citizens. We supply those in the rural areas with handouts so that they can survive and take care of their families. We cannot have a foreigner come here and decide for us. We will ensure that the man's lies are exposed. We know that the government's hand will touch him even if he goes to Britain. We have friends who can act on our behalf there. That is a malicious campaign against our country. You all know that there are good people who have helped our people through donations. Such people are welcome. We should applaud them and we hope they will not only help you but other people in rural areas," she continued.

"So my beloved people, when or let me say if it happens that such a person like this comes here, you should challenge him to provide an alternative. Even after relocation you will be free to come inside the reserve to collect whatever you might have forgotten. You cannot depend on gathering and hunting for your food. You need handouts. But we cannot provide them in the desert. You do not have to compete with wild animals. No, if you do you will end up, you know, doing... I hope you understand what I mean. Just imagine how the offspring would look like."

Suddenly a hand shot up. The Minister had to discontinue her monologue. She chuckled. She did not know whose hand it was, but she nodded and agreed with the owner of the hand to speak.

"I have only this message for you," said a young man with protruding teeth. "As soon as you take a flight back to Gaborone we will be packing our things and going straight home. This place is not where we belong."

Before the guests could know who the young man was, Jay held Jamana by the hand. If these two could disrupt court sessions, what about a meeting? They walked away from the meeting heading to Ghanzi, perhaps planning to disturb another court session.

# Chapter Sixteen

It has happened before in Africa that a man could be sponsored by foreign organizations to disturb peace in a country. Just imagine countries like Angola. Was Jay one of those men? The CKGR issue was now of interest to the people in the street. Now some men sat under a shade in Ghanzi and their conversation centred on the CKGR.

"I heard that the Minister of Foreign Affairs," said one of the men, "made an appeal to citizens of this country to consider their conscience in teaming up with foreigners. He said Jay should be warned that he should at least show respect to representatives of the government. He talked about the benefits of the relocation. What I also learnt is that Jay's reputation lost its steam when people, the guests, realised who really he was."

"That he is a Mosarwa?" queried Jamana.

"Yes," said another man. "It is said that they looked him up and down and knew. But others say that when he stood up, Jay's reputation rose beyond imagination like a whirlwind. This was when he said he would reveal the truth that led people to develop interest in the CKGR."

"Yes, it is said that he stressed: 'I demand respect first for my people,'" said another man. "You know what, Jay's voice was calm as if he talked to people he met on a daily basis. His reputation had grown like a day-old chick ever since his appearance on TV the previous week. Most people had never seen him and only knew his name, which appeared in newspapers focusing on the court case. Even the authorities did not know him. It was after he had appeared on TV that sometimes he made fun of the authorities by intentionally mispronouncing their names."

"But tell me," said another man. "Is it true that such courage has never been seen before?"

Jamana chuckled and nodded. "That is true."

One of the men nodded too. "Jay's actions have no match in this country."

"He is doing the right thing," added another one. "We need people who can say what bothers them without fear."

Jamana sighed and swallowed hard. "You know what? At first many people could not believe that we Basarwa could refuse development for free. People did not understand."

One of the men nodded in agreement. "It is even so. In fact no one did." The man paused and picked up a carton of a local brew, Chibuku.

Jamana smiled, then grinned. "People wondered; how could the Basarwa refuse things that people in other countries are dying for? Were developments not things that made people move from rural areas to cities and towns," they asked?

One of the men nodded. "Some people say Jay is being used. But who is using him since the authorities have established that he is one of us? Nevertheless, people are beginning to slowly recognize him."

The man holding the Chibuku could only agree in a murmur as the creamy contents were still in his mouth. He then added: "Do you know that some people have even started naming their children 'Jay,' not only here but also across the sea?"

"That is very interesting. At least we are being recognized after so many years," another one said.

"But there is one thing, Jamana," said another man. "People say that if the government concedes to Jay's demands, its reputation would suffer. Many citizens would do likewise. Where would the rule of law be? It would be ill-judgment."

Jamana chuckled and shrugged. "You know many stories are being told about Jay."

"That is true. He is a miracle," agreed one of the men.

"Even the authorities can't help it," said another. "There is a rumour spreading that Jay speaks English, his children go to expensive schools right here in Ghanzi and that he drives expensive cars."

"Some things may be true," the man paused. "Things can happen under our noses without us even being aware of them."

Jamana only chuckled, looking away and whistling to himself.

One man who had not said anything smiled. "No wonder Jay never flinches when speaking to the authorities. He knows what they know. He knows their secrets. I hear politicians and civic organizations look up to him these days."

The man continued: "He is said to have told newspaper people that, 'the authorities think I will give up. When my ancestral land, the CKGR calls, everyone, everything becomes a dwarf.'"

A man who had just joined the group chimed in: "I thought they would like the fight to continue because they have the resources at their disposal. 'I will fight with my bows and arrows to the bitter end,' he told the newspaper people."

One of the men picked up the Chibuku cartoon. "You know Jay compels everyone to listen. For it is said he holds terror for the authorities. It is also rumoured that his name only brings discomfort to those in power."

"'I can't use bows and arrows because by nature I come from a tribe that knows nothing about violence. They are the ones who started the fight,' he told the authorities," said another.

A young man wearing an American Football T-shirt said, "Jay told the Americans that, 'at home they say I would like to bring back colonialism in the country. This is because international human rights organizations want to assist me and my people. They say I'm exploiting my people through international human rights organizations. They say I'm betraying the struggle. Which struggle? I said at least I have not betrayed my people to multinational mining organizations which are piling what they get from the country into their mother countries.'"

Most of the men gathered under the shade of a Mongana tree in Ghanzi nodded as if they were confirming an old story that everybody knew. They wanted to know more about Jay from Jamana. And it was clear that they enjoyed the conversation.

"The educated, the elite, and the intellectuals have met their match in Jay."

"But we don't understand the role that is being played by Survival International, that is our confusion."

"What Survival International is doing," said another man raising his hands as though in a kind of rebelliousness, "is done in the belief that it is helping our people, nothing else."

Jamana stopped whistling and nodded. "People say that Jay invited foreigners into an issue that is supposed to involve us only."

Another man said, "What did the forefathers of this country do when the Boers wanted to take away the land before 1885?"

"But is it true," said another man, "that even babies in their mothers' bellies oppose the relocation? Some women are said to have miscarried in Kaudwane and New Xade."

Jamana shrugged and laughed. "It could be true."

"Some of those whose children were lucky to survive, named them Jay," continued the same man.

"I heard that," said another. "I heard that there are those among the authorities who admire his courage secretly."

"But is it not said that his wives and mother," said another man, "told him of the implications that his refusal to let people stay in the new settlements would have on the

CKGR residents? Such a mighty power like government! With its people who always wear suits even when it is hot! People tell me that the senior wife, Xhwaashe, was worried. They say that even as she cooked eland meat at New Xade that Jay had brought one day, her mind refused to stay on the task at hand," he paused for breath and continued.

"Sometimes, people said, she felt that she had wanted to agree with the relocation. They say that she had a feeling that trouble was coming and her body had communicated that to her. It is said that only yesterday she dreamed herself fetching water in a basket only to find it full of mud."

"But Jay is determined," said Jamana. "He would rather see people suffer than surrender to the authorities' demands."

One of the men shook his head. "But I tend to agree with those who say that Jay has been promised money by foreigners."

Jamana nodded. Then he said: "That is what people say." He paused, surveying the men with twinkling eyes. "People can no longer believe the story that Jay is continuing to oppose the relocation."

"But Jamana is it true that the authorities are wondering where Jay gets the money for legal expenses?" Jamana shrugged and looked away. "It could be true. There is nothing one should take lightly these days. I am told the authorities want to investigate where the money comes from."

Another man nodded. "We told Jay to let the people relocate as they wish but he would not hear of it because foreigners from their countries are misleading him. These foreigners have told him that the ancestors' place would be for diamond prospecting which will only fatten the pockets of the already wealthy."

Jamana nodded again. "Exactly what I heard." Another man chuckled. "One of the leaders also said, 'sometimes I agree with those who say that the man is not a Mosarwa.

How could he let his people suffer and be used by tourists who are interested in their pictures? Such a man does not have his people's interest at heart."

"But I grew up With Jay," said Jamana. "And l know him better than most people do. Why would he refuse people to relocate if there is no grain of truth he wants to share with the world?"

"It is like that," said another. "If you go to Gaborone and stay there working, would you want the whole family to come there? At times people talk as if they are the only ones who have senses and words. People in different towns are from various places but you cannot argue that they have no place to call home."

"But is it not true that Jay had been looking for ways," said another, "to make money after leaving the mines in South Africa?" Jamana did not respond to this. He only smiled again.

"It could be true," said another. "It is also said that Survival International organization saw the CKGR case as an opportunity that presented itself with its background of speaking on behalf of minority groups, and it grabbed the opportunity."

"But we have tried to dialogue with our own leaders," said Jamana. "With the assistance of Ditshwanelo, WIMSA... but because of the historical contempt that has been passed down by past generations, they looked at us and laughed. So they should not blame Jay but rather their pride and arrogance."

The arrival of two men interrupted the speaker.

"Have you heard the latest news?"

"What is it Boikobo?"

"If you have some relatives in the CKGR please rush there now," said Boikobo panting for breath and still gasping for air.

"Why, what has happened?" Several men demanded to know simultaneously. Boikobo hesitated like a hen laying eggs for the first time would do when looking for a new nest.

"They have cut the source of livelihood." Boikobo paused as if the memories of what he was talking about were still fresh in his mind.

Then he spoke up. "People say that this will be the living evidence that the government is the custodian of its citizens, not foreign organizations. They also wonder what human rights Jay is looking for. Why can't he read the constitution? Is that constitution not from Britain, the very country that Jay is looking for rights from?"

No one spoke. Boikobo seemed to recover from shock as he continued speaking. But there was still pain in his voice.

"The residents of CKGR are confused now," he said. "Some are suspecting that they have been misled by Jay. They say all along the authorities were right. Was the water not part of the development and resources that the authorities spoke of in their meetings after the relocation? The very resources that it wanted the residents of CKGR to enjoy..." Boikobo paused again and shook his head.

"'Let Jay provide you with the resources," said Boikobo, "because you decided to listen to his advice, one leader was heard to have said as the people looked at him like children would at an adult dangling a fruit." Still no one spoke.

The arrival of Boikobo and the latest news seemed to have sealed their mouths. They appeared to have abandoned the Chibuku.

Boikobo continued speaking. "The cutting off of the water summed up everything, that government is in control and is the custodian of the people. Everyone must adhere to its orders. It is the parent of its citizens. What power does Jay have to tell the people not to listen to their mighty parent, the government? How could he shout in front of the authorities like that? Where did he get that power?"

Several men let out deep sighs.

"Meanwhile, the dancing in the CKGR has suffered a blow," said Boikobo. "You know that this was the month for the trance dance. People who have returned there wore sad faces. Jay has become a bullet with which foreigners want to destroy peace and our democracy. Such an alarm people say, has not been known in living memory, not even when Ian Smith used to threaten people living along the Zimbabwean border in the 1980s."

"Tell us something different," said Jamana. "Where is Jay himself?"

"Yes, where is Jay?" asked three more men at the same time. It was as if they sensed betrayal in Boikobo's words.

"Just as the people were beginning to learn a lesson," said Boikobo, "and the authorities were watching with glee, celebrating the termination of services in CKGR, Jay and Survival International had other plans."

Boikobo was interrupted by the arrival of three police officers riding horses. With them was Jay. A day earlier, Jamana observed, Jay would not walk around without the eland horns. Was Boikobo telling the truth that they were about to lose everything? Even Jay's horns? He had no time to reflect on this as he was also quickly handcuffed.

# Chapter Seventeen

It was a day after his release from prison. Jay sat on a cross-legged stool and stared into space. Some people have done it. They have led their people to their lands. It was not something new. It has happened before. He was not the first one to do it. In fact, he would never be the last. Moses did it according to the Bible. If a man of God could do it, why couldn't he? He was not a sinner. The sinner was the one who wanted to take his home, steal his people.

He tried to open his mouth, to say something. But hot saliva again spread in his throat and swallowed it with his words. He tilted his head against the wall of his already dilapidating hut as he watched the sun almost being swallowed by huge clouds in the south. The sun seemed stuck in the same spot. It was crawling at a snail's pace and appeared dull and blood-stained.

He craned his neck a little and saw a van parking outside. The police! A middle aged man was behind the wheel and he took his time to alight. Perhaps preparing the handcuffs, Jay thought. At last Jay sighed, relieved as he recognized who the driver of the other van was. Jamana parked the van outside the compound. After exchanging greetings, he plunged straight into the subject of his visit.

"When will you be ready?"

This question confirmed that indeed Jay had agreed that he would lead the people back to CKGR again. Perhaps for the last time. He had signed a contract with them. Jay could have fainted when he heard this question as he had secretly changed his mind again not to resist relocation or try to locate his missing people. But he was drained of all the little energy he had from the wild goose meat that morning. He was weary. In that condition he was too old to rise, he thought.

"There must be someone else to do it this time, Jamana." Jay unexpectedly found his mouth open. It was a pointless suggestion. He knew. Had he not spoken strongly about refusing to relocate and finding the missing people? Was there someone bribing him now?

He was depressed and felt lonely. With the creeping in of this loneliness Jay knew he would not do it. He would not lead the people back home or find his missing people. He could not. No more days of this.

Jay did not want to talk. Not about the CKGR, anyway. Jamana asked another question. But Jay was not listening. He did not hear him. He did not understand the question itself. When he raised his head from the walls of his hut, he saw a group of people outside.

"Jay let Ditshwanelo handle the issue," said Lere thinking that the people outside were indeed police officers.

"They know better. They know most of the things that you and I, or anyone of our people don't. Remember that they helped the two men who were about to be hanged."

"No, I can't!" Jay said unexpectedly, to everyone's surprise.

"But Ditshwanelo could help us because they know many people. They have connections within the government. Survival International is using our people just like tourists who normally come here and take our pictures."

Jay looked at his father. "I can't accept that." He sneezed.

"Remember that at first when we wanted to go home, even the court said I could not speak on behalf of my people. It dismissed the case on the grounds that I couldn't speak on behalf of my people."

Jamana shook his head and licked his thin lips. "But that was a different matter. There are procedures to follow when launching a court application, Jay."

"But the court only believed our voice when we brought Benny in. Only because he is from Britain."

"Or Phoko because he has book learning," said another young man.

There was silence.

"You know everyone in this country is talking about you," said Jay's mother, Mawee.

"They say if a Mosarwa can do it, why can't we? For the first time Jay, people say that the Basarwa can do it."

Jay did not respond but only whistled quietly. He looked away from his audience and gazed down trying to hide his curiosity. Jamana left him and went outside the compound to the group assembled outside.

"What is happening?"he asked his son, Ndowe. The boy rushed outside. There were more than a hundred people outside Jay's compound, women, men and children. There were also more than ten vans. Ndowe ran back to his father.

"Come and see, father," Ndowe said.

"What is it?" Jay asked his mind having gone to the police and wildlife officers and away from Ditshwanelo.

"People." Ndowe was excited and afraid simultaneously like a woman giving birth for the first time.

"Which  people?" asked Jay. He strengthened his back and fastened his eland horns. He passed his youngest wife's hut and went outside the compound. The people cheered when they saw him. Surprised, Jay stopped, unable to comprehend the scene before him. Jamana was about to explain but he was interrupted by the voices of the people.

"Our Moses take us away from this Egypt," said a young man, "this new settlement and deliver us back to our Canaan, our CKGR."

Suddenly, a song broke. It was the youth who took over the song from the young man.

"Moses, Moses... Go to Egypt and Deliver My People to The Land of Israel I heard Lord... But I'm Afraid... To Go To Egypt And Deliver... Because Pharaoh is a cruel Man..."

It was Jamana and other young men who responded to the young women, the leading vocalists. Jay just stood there. He had to listen. But he did not understand. Then Jamana turned to him.

"Do you understand what they are requesting from you?" Jay shrugged his shoulders and his eyes narrowed.

A chuckle escaped Jamana's lips. "It is the story of a man of the God of Jews, Moses, in their history book which is also known as the Bible. What he did is exactly what you must do now. Take these people back to where they belong, their country." Jay shook his head. But there was a glimpse of light in his eyes.

"Lace up your shoes," Jay said unexpectedly again. "We are going back to....you said the place is called what in the Bible?"

"To our Israel, CKGR," the youth shouted.

The elderly people rested with their heads supported by their hands. Whether they understood or not, they seemed not to care. All they wanted was to be delivered to the CKGR.

"Those with babies," Jay shouted "prepare your backs as your babies should be strapped now. We do not know what lies ahead. Expect to lose your lives." Jay's family had joined the group now. The people set out in the vans. As the journey started off the voices died down. Jay was at war with his mind. It was filled with evil; to kill at any cost. His hands itched, almost ached. He was ready to kill whoever stood in his way to find his missing people. It was something to be done straight away, a dream to be fulfilled. This dream emptied his mind. His mind registered nothing. Empty like a vessel to be filled with a need. In the place of the dream there was a vision; finding his people became a mixture of vision and need.

Not a want. The love for the land turned into hate. He was possessed. He was obsessed with the need to find his people. The authorities would never see their dreams. Whatever their plans about the land were, he would censor them. The reflection was terrifying. It was so exciting and fresh that it stung him like a new experience. He found it strange after he had taken the last decision - not to go back to the CKGR or find his missing people. A thought of another kind crept in.

Perhaps he was dreaming. Jay wished there had never been this belief, this belief that other tribes were superior to others. A belief that the inferior could be controlled and their responses allowed at a pace set by their superiors.

Jay knew that failing to find an answer to a question was only a dream, a wish. It was like an extremely undesirable beast recoiling inside his head; an illusion completely bad for his health.

He prayed that there had never been a gap between the rich and the poor, leaders and their servants. Then he would never have been sent by the gods to find his people or lead his missing people. But the obsession to go back home was rushing all over his hair, his knees, his bones and the tip of his fingers. His feet itched again. Then he remembered that he had not taken his bows and arrows, in case the security agents engaged him in a fight. The thought that yesterday the authorities were urging people to relocate made him put away the bows and arrows and take out his gun to match the development and civilization that he was resisting. He told Jamana to increase the van's speed.

By the time Jay and his people reached the GKGR entrance, the heavenly watcher, the lonely silent witness who could not testify against him, the sun, was already in the middle of the sky. It was afternoon, scorching and very hot.

Today, after his legs had carried him into the CKGR, into its shrubs and mixture of sandy dunes, everyone would know from the news bulletin that he was in CKGR. Everyone including the British Prince, without having to respond to his letter, would know that his people had gone back to living like before, hunting and gathering and dancing.

People would know that he was an honest leader, a leader serving his people. They would know. People would understand. With this thought possessing his entire mind the loneliness crept in again. A mixture of warmth and cold pierced his heart like a sword. Why did he leave Jamana and the people behind in the vans? Did he want to show the world how determined he was?

He had to be in the CKGR before his dreams, his people's visions could be crushed by the arms of government. His knees seemed to knock against each other despite his wide rickets that indicated the good runner he was in his youth.

Perhaps this was because of the number of the security agents at the gate. He nearly collided with a man carrying wild fruits and hurriedly passed him without exchanging greetings. The man also looked at him and said nothing. At the gate he nearly made a quick turn, but something at the far end of his brain advised him to keep on walking. But where exactly was he going? Before he could find a solution to this question another man called out to him and approached him.

Jay halted. And the man stopped too. The man motioned him to come to him. Jay's legs continued their briefly interrupted journey.

It was when Jay raised his head to see who was shouting at him when he felt, rather than saw, that this was a police officer. He hesitated. Not sure whether to stop or move on. A wave of shock crept into his head, muscles, hands, almost everywhere. His eyes grew bigger like a week old baby. When the policeman shouted a second time, something like ice melted in his bowels so that it nearly defrosted his rigid intestines.

The ground below shook. It was loose and unsteady. The policeman shouted.

"Are you deaf?" he asked.' "I said come over here." Jay let out a sigh and resolutely followed the direction he had come from. The man he had seen when he approached the gate was still there. He was a tall man, imposing, manipulating. It seemed he was the one who was now calling him. But the police man who had called him ordered him to stop.

"One more step and I'll blow out your brain!" he shouted.

"Yes," Jay agreed. But he heard nothing, saw nothing. He was alone again.

Jay could not see the police who were busy chatting at the CKGR gate. The shrubs were silent as usual. But he could not see them. It was only him and the CKGR. His home. He turned and faced the police officer and went to him. The semi sunken Kalahari sun seemed to give him more energy. It was moderately hot now.

He looked at the sun and realized with indignation that he had wasted a lot of time in cooperating with the gods in the CKGR. Suddenly, a voice burning and demanding like a new experience and in harmony with the CKGR ordered him to surrender to the gods' calling. He was supposed to stop a meeting that was on in the CKGR, again for those who had gone back stealthily. He had to disrupt it. He had to tell his people not to be misled.

Jay nodded his head. He had heard his people's call, but before he could do anything he found himself surrounded by hundreds of security agents. By now the other people who accompanied him, came out of the vans and joined him. Some women still with babies strapped on their backs.

"Dismiss at once."

It was a command. And Jay thought he heard Sennye's voice. But this was a different one; with traces of a man trained to command, a soldier. The people chanted songs.

"We want to go home! We want to go home!"

They were approaching the gate and tourists who wanted to go in and out had discontinued their journeys. It was a sight to behold. The revolution was near at hand. Suddenly there was a deafening silence. Smoke covered the beautiful blue Kalahari sky, contaminating it. Terror was unleashed. The women with the babies shouted in panic. The whips that descended on Jay's body were countless.

"The man is mad," one of the agents said. "Take him to Lobatse Mental Hospital."

At least five security agents and three wildlife officials ran to the scene. It was a scene that remained a dream to him. It was not a nightmare. When the security agents descended on him, Jay did not feel the torture. It was not pain he felt but joy. He did not see them. Instead he heard the pleading cries of his people. Many voices were begging him. Voices of his mother and people were troubling him. Suddenly everything around him was enveloped in darkness. "Arrest him," the senior security agent said. He then went to Jay and put his army boots on him, as he lay on the ground.

"And definitely you will have to return those horns. Where did you get these other ones? I mean last time they were taken away from you? There is only one government here. I mean, how will the country be if everyone wants to be the president or if others say they want two governments? We don't want anarchy here. This is not the USA where you have states. We have learnt that you assembled even foreigners from overseas to come here claiming that they should help you locate your lost people and that you want your people to be visible. The spectacles that you are wearing, can't they help you see your people even if you are with them?"

The officer turned to his men.

"Throw them inside the van now and back to jail before he disrupts an ongoing meeting at the new settlements, being addressed by important and visible people."

# Chapter Eighteen

"We shall bring more resources to you." The man was fat. A small ball comprised his head. His eyes were wide apart and seemed to burst out of their eyelids. His nose was wide and as he spoke, his meaty hands went up and down as if the people before him were a choral choir.

"You cannot stay like before," he continued. "So I have been sent to let you know of the benefits that will be given to you, more than what you have already received... and this place New Xai..."

"Xade," a young woman corrected him.

"Yes, Xaaade."

The fat man laughed as if the laughter would correct the mistake. His chest heaved.

"As I was saying," he continued deeply, "we have moved you to this place so that the government can provide you with resources when you are closer to other citizens."

"What are resources?" An elderly woman wanted to know. Unlike in the first meeting, people were now able to ask questions. Perhaps it was because of Jay's persuasive words. All the people's eyes were on the government man's eyes. It seemed they had been eager to know what resources were. The fat government man seemed to enjoy the monopoly he had on the knowledge of resources. He retreated with laughter and placed his hand on his face to wipe away the perspiration forming. The Kalahari sun was anchored in the middle of the sky and the man looked at his own shadow, only to be met by a disfigured outline. There were no details, no shape, only the shadow of a huge Morula tree stump with the shadow of a ball on top.

"Resources, you know," he said, "are things like, you know, food, clothes, education, just to mention a few."

It seemed the former residents of the CKGR had expected

something new or something that they had not seen from some of their people or tourists. They laughed, but there was a man among them who remained unmoved. He had a sad face and appeared despondent. An old man sitting close to him repeated the question that had been asked before.

"Which is this government you speak of?" asked the old man. "Do you mean Rayzo Khai or another man?"

Rayzo Khai was a Member of Parliament for the area under which the CKGR fell.

"He is part of the government," the fat man said. His voice now calm. He had adopted a serious tone. "Now, whoever wants something clarified should identify himself," said the government man. Perhaps he had not expected the questions and they made him uneasy. Could it be that there were people still bent on resisting relocation? People who wanted to spoil the development plans that the CKGR residents were to get? But news had reached him that Jay had been arrested at the CKGR gate. What was there now to be feared?

"As I was saying," he continued. "I would like you to also be the eyes of the government because you are part of the government."

There was silence.

With the silence he had created, the man's voice rose and he was unable to control his anger. Something was swelling within him.

"You can't be staying in these tiny shacks where only your heads fit. So many children are sharing the same shack; no way my good people. I mean, you have privacy. You, I mean you, when you want to... you know what I mean and your children watching. We also want you to be part of this lovely nation. We want you to start enjoying the fruits of independence like other citizens, since 1966 citizens have enjoyed that at your expense. I don't need to tell you that your time has come. You know we nearly forgot that you people existed, or should I say, we were unable to see you. Now the scales have fallen from our eyes and we can see you," he paused to wipe away perspiration.

"We want you to contribute to the development of the country. And that can only be possible when you move out of this place. I have never in my life come across a place as bad as this. You know, Europeans when they come to our country they normally say, 'hey you, the authorities, why do you ill-treat your fellow men. You Africans, we have civilized you, and now it's time to pass that to your fellow men.' Some of them even suggest that you are not real human beings. But we want to show them that they are liars. In fact, we have reassured them that our fellow men, the Basarwa, adopt to change slowly. We even threatened to take them to the International criminal court if they kept on calling you Bushmen. The best way to stop them is to relocate you so that if they keep calling you that, we will warn them that you no longer stay in the Bush. We don't need their assistance to relocate you-this is between the authority and its citizens. Again they wanted to teach us how we should run our country. All these years we knew that a time would come when you would want to relocate and embrace civilization, development and benefit from our minerals that the British are jealous of. We are not the ones who said that they should fail to detect the rich minerals that we had when they colonized us. You will agree with me, good people, that this is the right time to take you out of the Dark Ages. We even reassured foreigners, particularly Europeans and Americans, that the Basarwa, I mean you, that nothing will be left behind. Everything will be relocated. Your bows and arrows, your languages, your culture, even your foot prints." At this stage in his speech the residents who were quiet all along began to murmur among themselves.

"It's possible these days," the fat man reassured his audience. "We are living in the world of technology. This means that nothing is impossible because we have all the knowledge that there is to do everything. And you know the whole world has always questioned how a democratic country like ours could oppress its people by leaving them behind in the desert. Indeed, we don't believe in separate development. This is not the old South Africa. We would not like to remind our neighbours of such things when they hear that you are in a world of your own. I mean in this desert. Let those who want to divide us go and destroy their parents' marriage. Good people, let's sing the same song. After all we come from the same womb. We might not speak the same language, practice the same culture or differ in physical structures, but we come from the same egg. Even the hen's chicks don't look alike. But they are from the same hen. Who knows, maybe a son from this place will be the president in future. It's possible. But he needs education. He has to be educated in all the schools in the world, starting from elementary education here and then tertiary education in Europe. There, he will learn about what democracy really is, how to manage the country's economy and even his own business. I mean, good people, we can't have a president who doesn't even know the latest price of drinking water or a leader who gets lost in another country."

This did not go down well with the residents. The last part, where the men mentioned that water was sold, confirmed their suspicions that the relocation was going to complicate their lives. It was going to bring disaster. A lot of things would be destroyed. But since they were thirsty, they did not want to talk about water as this brought memories of good days in the reserve before the water supply was cut off. Things would never be the same again. Had the water pumps not been cut already in CKGR? But the fat man managed to silence them with his sweet talk. If you want to rob a monkey of its baby, you must throw some crumbs and it will definitely let the baby in its arms go. At this stage, the foam was drooling from the fat man's mouth.

"Good people," he said licking his lips. "If you think that

this layer of fat that has disfigured me is from wild fruits and wild animals' meal, you will have to search your mind again. Where I come from, rather let me put it this way, this place, this new settlement is almost the same as where I come from. You don't eat the same food every day there. There you eat non-stop like a Mophane worm. You can eat until you swell. It depends on how much your stomach is able to accommodate. It also depends on what shape you want. You may eat so that your hands, limbs and feet disappear. Why do you think my head had shrunk from the size of a full moon to a fist? And good people, your daily routine of dust settling in your throat as a result of chasing an eland will come to an end. Let me also hasten to say that even the trance dance whereby you people jump and fall into fire and sustain major injuries would come to an end. Here in New Xade you will watch movies and television. I mean, where you have just been relocated to. No more wailing all night long alone. There you assemble and pray at a building called church. We have only one God, people. We don't need to be divided. No seeds of division should be sworn. Though modern life has its delights, it does not come cheap. You will have to find employment and start to pay bills, taxes and so forth. But the good thing is that when you want to answer the call of nature, you do not have to rush into the bush and at times fail to relieve yourself because you fear a lion might pounce on you any time. With civilization and development, you do it in the same house. I know that some of you might think that this is impossible, but as I mentioned, nothing is impossible in this era."

"As I was saying, it is in the best interest of our country and other citizens to relocate you closer to other citizens of this country," he said again wiping away perspiration.

But how could someone come and tell the former residents of the CKGR that they were part of the government rather that they were the government itself? No, doubt education had gone to his head. He should leave them alone. Some of them complained that the man had wasted their time. That they could have gathered more wild fruits in the CKGR rather than sitting here in New Xade doing nothing.

The old woman who had asked a question stood up, half erect. She put her other hand on her back as if to straighten it up, but only drooped further and began speaking in that position.

She was the same old woman who had wanted to know about the government. Now she was on her feet, as if to remind the fat man that he was not there to play games.

"You said we are part of the government. How?" She wanted to know. Some people glanced at her and giggled. Indeed new things were coming into the Reserve.

"It's people like you that vote some people into power," said the government man. "If it was not for your votes we would not have a government, and those people would not wield any power. It is also from you that the people you have voted get ideas. These people represent you. They represent your thoughts, your... you know... The Government of the people by the people. Hence, you are part of the Government. You will learn about this as we bring you close to civilization and development."

"But if what you are saying is true," the old woman placed her hand over her forehead as if to help her sight, "the idea of relocation did not come from us. It is something new to us. We never initiated that. And I understand no one here was willing to relocate. I mean, how can we leave our soil, our wild fruits and not to mention our snakes and our ancestors' graves?"

She sat and crossed her legs, her words earning her a standing ovation from the audience gathered at the meeting. The fat man smiled and seemed to move forward, a step or two. He looked at the Mosu tree under which some residents sat with their babies clasped in their arms. They had made a circle around the tree.

Although some of them were young, the majority was

made up of elders. These were people who had not joined others when Jay and other people were arrested at the CKGR gate.

"That does not mean that the ideas will always come from you," explained the fat man. "People, you have to understand how a government works. And you will. For instance, some of the things are called government programs, in English, what is called a manifesto of the party."

The man raised his voice unnecessarily, but one thing was clear. He was impatient with these people who did not understand even a single word of his speech, though he spoke Setswana, a national language that some of them understood.

"As for the question of leaving some of your things behind in CKGR. As I mentioned earlier, everything should have been loaded. Even your ancestors' graves if you can't live without them."

"But you said the people we voted represented our ideas and thoughts." The same old woman was back again. Some people laughed.

"Yes, as I mentioned before," said the fat man. "Sometimes the leaders, your leaders, have to formulate ideas and come up with plans without consulting you. They will then consult you later."

"No," said the old woman, "but you said we should move out of this place. You did not ask us if we agree with your plan to relocate from this reserve. After all, you are not our representative. How will you understand our aspirations? In fact, when we saw a fat man we did not believe that people like you still existed. We thought you were part of those man-eaters in folklores. Had it not been for some of us who have been to your places."

"But that is not important, old woman," the fat man now could not hide his anger.

"Listen here, the most important thing is..." The fat man coughed. Some people stood up. He looked this way and that way. He had to finish before the people dispersed otherwise his bosses would be angry with him. He ordered his men to bring some boxes from two trucks that were parked close to where the people gathered. From the trucks the man's officials showered the people with clothes, sweets, food, school materials, blankets and almost every household item. The people staying around areas in the second city, Francistown, would have hated this. Was it not a documented fact that their land now belonged to European mining companies which bought them with sweets from their chiefs hundreds of years ago?

"We have been given those things." A young man said as the fat man rushed around colliding with his officers in an effort to stop some former CKGR residents who were already on their way to their newly built homes. He told them that all those things belonged to them. And more of those things, rather things bigger than those were to be provided when they had settled in the new settlements. As if not to be outdone, the fat man ordered his men to take out more things. He even took out some radios and wanted to offer one to the old woman who had engaged him in a verbal war.

"I can't take something that is not mine. That would be stealing..." Before the old woman could finish her sentence the fat man took out another parcel wrapped in a small box, handling it with care if it was a precious item. This prompted the old woman to ask with disdain:

"What is it?"

There was a grain of interest in the old woman's voice which she failed to conceal from her listeners.

"It is for family planning," said the fat man. "That is to say, for controlling the number of babies that one wants to have. The unwanted baby would be trapped in this thing and stop it from going in to the woman's...oh good people, you know what I'm talking about."

The fat man had now taken out the thing he was talking about. He was about to demonstrate how the thing was used, when the old woman asked him another question.

"You use it yourself?"

The fat man was happy that at least the old woman showed interest.

"Yes, this thing is like my shadow," he explained further. "It is always there. I use it almost every day, and good people, I only have two children." He looked around like someone who had misplaced a precious item in a dangerous place. He found a walking stick. But the old woman rushed there and took it away from him.

The fat man looked around again and found one which did not belong to anyone. He tore the cover of the thing in his hand and removed it quickly as people watched him, murmuring. He unrolled the thing on the stick and began demonstrating as if he was doing the real deed. Some people, especially those with grey hair shook their heads. This seemed immoral. Others laughed and the fat man smiled thinking that people had received the message. But they laughed. Not because of the number of children the man had, but because they imagined such a big man on top of his wife using the thing. Or the man with his large overlapping tummy there with his wife watching him putting on the thing he was talking about.

"This thing is called a condom," the fat man explained, "You know, don't you, that there is another dangerous and unfriendly disease called HIV/AIDS? That disease can smile at you before sex, knowing that if you don't use this, you will die." And here, the man lifted the condom in the air for the people to see. Some were standing at a distance from where the fat man was as if they did not want him to infect them with the strange disease he spoke of and which they did not know. They gathered again, but at a safe distance. The man in his explanation spoke very fast like someone about to be hanged.

"Do you mean syphilis?" It was the same old woman. "That one we can cure." The old woman looked at the other officials under the blue tent as though directing her words at them not the fat man. On both sides of the fat man were three officials dressed in the same dark blue uniforms as the fat man. There were also two police officers. A large table on which the 'resources' were displayed formed the boundary between the officials and the former residents of the CKGR.

"No, no, this one is a new disease," the fat man explained.

"It has no cure. It is transmitted through sex like the disease you just mentioned now, but it strikes like a deadly poisonous mamba that is common in the CKGR. The difference is that you can kill the mamba, but this disease..."

The old woman stared at the fat man for some time as if she would insult his parents. It was as if it was only the two of them at the meeting.

"You are right. You are also new," she said. "You seem not to understand our ways, now you want to bring things that would destroy us. So, I would suggest that we remain ancient, without your resources. At least with our ancient things, including our old diseases and mambas we can cure and kill. To the best of my knowledge there is no disease that cannot be cured here. I have already known that your new things were destructive."

Several people burst into laughter again, but this was a painful, touching laughter. Even some officials smiled at this. Only the old woman and the fat man did not join in the laughter.

"These things trap a man's seeds..." said the fat man.

"Those seeds are meant to go where they are supposed to go," the old woman cut him short.

"Now you see. The disease you have just talked about. It was born because of new things. Too much change. You change too many things without considering the impact. This new generation! Who knows? What is it that you want in our land?" She paused and then continued: "Many lies. You tell lies. Every word that comes out of your mouth I can hardly believe it. You are like Kganu, a friend to the wild cat. He is said to have told him that he should not enter a hole which he had been using, and which was given to him by his ancestors since time immemorial. Kganu told the wild cat that there was a snake in his hole. But when the wild cat left the hole and opted for a tree, who did he find when he came back after the tree he was resting on was gutted by fire? None other than Kganu."

As she said these words, the old woman pointed at the heavens with her walking stick as if asking the gods to be her witnesses. At last, she pointed at the fat man as if showering him with curses. Her voice was abrasive and there was a terrifying twinkle in her eyes. She stood up and paused a moment as if there was another thought lingering on her mind.

"You spoke of wild animals being dangerous to our lives," she continued. "The question I would like to ask is: are there no wild animals where you come from?"

Here she stopped. She seemed to wait for an answer. The fat man and his colleagues did not answer her. They only listened. Suddenly the fat man began addressing the people again, ignoring the old woman.

But the people were not listening anymore. They were talking among themselves. They were talking about the old woman Qoero, an elder. Something bad was going to happen and it was on its way.

"I always felt in my nerves and blood that something ominous was going to come." Those were her last words.

People feared for the future. What was it that even old Qoero feared? Resolutely, the old woman pointed her stick to the heavens once again and spat on the cracked sandy soil before going away.

"We will come and tell you when to start doing things, rather, we will come and teach you about modern lifestyles," the fat man sneezed. "Before I forget, you will also have to rear cattle. We will give you the cattle and goats...money..."

A hand shot up. The fat man was taken aback, as he had not finished his words. He looked this way and that way.

"Okay," he said at last. "Let's hear what you have to say. And please, before you say anything, introduce yourself."

"What I would like to know...Ok let me..." the man who had raised his hand said.

"I said you must introduce yourself first," the fat man said impatiently.

"I'm Jay's..." Before the man could finish, he was interrupted by the fat man.

"Police, do what you have been trained to do."

At least four police men pounced on the man who had wanted to introduce himself.

The fat man sighed and it echoed into the wilderness, thunder. He was at a loss.

Was Jay not arrested this morning? Those policemen and wildlife officials at the gate, had they released him already. Or had they arrested the wrong person? In the confused atmosphere, he fished out a radio from his pocket.

"Hello, caller," he bellowed into the radio. "Have you released Jay already?" He was silent for a moment as he listened to the voice at the end of the line and shook his head.

"He is here," he said. "He nearly disrupted the meeting had we not acted in time." He paused again to listen to the other speaker's voice.

The fat man shrugged his shoulders. "Perhaps you have arrested the wrong man. If indeed you still have that man in prison, release him, Jay is here. We made sure that he was arrested."

That instant, the man who had raised his hand was escorted to a van nearby. He was thrown into the van. Jay's reputation had ruined the meeting. Was it true that he was from the Kalahari Desert?

# Chapter Nineteen

The next couple of months were the happiest Jay had ever dreamt of. He would lie under a Mosu tree close to his hut in Ghanzi hoping and fearing for the future. He was happy because he had talked to the owner of Kuru Development Trust and Lillian, the leader of Ditshwanelo, the Centre for Human Rights. They had both pledged to help him and his people go back to the CKGR or even find the people he said he was looking for. He knew that they would help him. Everything was under control again. He had no expenses. Everything would be paid for. But at the same time he feared for his people. There were enemies and friends. Some people did not support his people's wish to go back home. But for such people he did not care; in fact, he did not mind. Why should he? But sometimes as if in a nightmare his stomach would be gripped, trapped in a cage.

Remembering the torture at the hands of wildlife officials, waiting for tomorrow, for the future to come, he thought of requesting Survival International to launch the latest bullet. However, he resolved to wait for Lillian and Drum to call on him. But sometimes his mood, his thoughts, would seem new or foreign to him as if he had not agreed with Ditshwanelo, Kuru and WIMSA for possible negotiation with the government. It was agreed that he was the leader of his people, agreed that he would represent their aspirations come what may. Was this true? Could this be real? He kept on thinking "I must be mad, need to be taken to Lobatse Mental Hospital." What right did he, a Mosarwa, have to be a representative of a lost people? There was no need to look far; South African history on its own confirmed the suspicion that he was mad.

The Basarwa had no leaders, had no voice and were

always on the move. How then could he oppose the leaders' decision to relocate them particularly when they were invisible? If constant migration was indeed their way of life as written by historians, what right, or who was he to say no to relocation?

Jay knew that if he could think of the CKGR issue as a useless, meaningless thing, the whole stupid idea of his madness as a leader of the Basarwa would leave his mind, disappear, vanish like any other unimportant thought. But the idea that three weeks ago Drum and Lillian had opposed the relocation, had joined him and his people, had seen that it was important to protest, made him realize that it was true he was a leader. He desperately wanted to help his people.

Jay had never thought about his position before. The Kalahari Desert in which he had spent his days as a boy before joining other Batswana men at the South African mines, was full of Basarwa tribes who had been pushed from rich lands long ago and settled in the desert, probably longer than any other people. These various groups comprised of the Gana and Gwi, who may have migrated from as far as the present day Cape Town in South Africa. This was the result of historical events such as the Mfecane wars between the Africans and the Great Trek by the Boers. They still kept their languages and practiced their customs; hunting and gathering. Nobody bothered them. Even Jay himself grew up as a hunter.

But growing up like that would not stop him from being a leader, he reflected. Some people grew up herding cattle but became heads of state, like his favourite hero, Nelson Mandela. He would feel terribly upset when the thought of allowing his people to stay forever in the new settlements struck him. Even as he sat in Ghanzi under the shade of his hut, after Phoko had secured his release from prison, he would gaze past the Savannah shrubs, past the plain sand dunes. His mood would shift to the present thinking of Drum, itching to see him. So clear was the picture of Drum that he felt a bitter longing. Drum spoke Setswana fluently without a nasal tone like Benny. Sometimes they would spend the whole day talking, sometimes waiting for Lillian to come. Jay would catch both Drum and Lillian looking at him, and himself looking at Drum more than at Lillian. Perhaps because Drum had more power over him as a man than the woman.

Lillian would look with envy and admiration as the two men talked with a mixture of worry and confusion. Drum and Lillian also had the same smiles, difficult for Jay to resist. So powerful were their smiles that Jay could not understand them. He did not know, did not understand if Drum wanted him to join in smiling along with them. But at the same time he was also confused by Lillian with her diamond teeth shining more as it met the Kalahari sun and her relaxed smile. He knew that he had to please those two. His thoughts had to flow with theirs, be at one with theirs.

At times he would wonder though, what was beyond those smiles? Why had the rights of the Basarwa become so important to Lillian and Drum now and even some churches. They had not explained, as that organization from Britain, Survival International and the Prince had done in the letter which he had to show them. The question would leave his mind blank, empty and drowned. Then these two friends of his would rise and leave him still confused, before he could find possible answers to his own questions.

Did the negotiating team really care about the Basarwa's rights? Were they sincere in their promises? There was one incident which seemingly proved to Jay that they cared. He did not want to lose them too. And they also did not want to lose him for various security reasons, physical emotions.

The incident confirming their sincerity happened when one day Jay's crocodile tooth necklace fell on the table at a meeting organized by the negotiating team at Gaborone

Sun. That day Lillian and Drum nearly collided rushing for the crocodile necklace as much as they were hurrying to help the former residents of CKGR, Jay thought.

Drum had looked at Jay after Lillian had handed over the necklace. He smiled as if weighing Jay up and down: the stunted hair, the speckled, unshaven beard, Jay's pointed ears. The closeness of the eyes which seemed to have been squeezed and those lips which appeared inadequate to cover the teeth. The tight facial skin as if the owner was experiencing an unexpected anguish, almost clear enough for the muscles to be seen. The medium height. To Drum, everything about Jay left no doubt as to his ethnicity. Jay was typical of what historians had said were Basarwa's characteristics, Drum reflected. So it could not be said all European historians were liars. Even Sarah Baartman, the woman stolen from Cape Town and used as an exhibit in Europe, shared characteristics with Jay, Drum had reflected. But people still asked themselves, was Jay from the desert? This question at times also haunted him, and he was still asking himself the same question when he dozed off, waiting for Jamana.

# Chapter Twenty

A few days after meeting Drum and Lillian, Jay and Jamana decided to go back to the CKGR. They had the full support of Drum and Lillian. Oh, and he had forgotten so soon, Survival International. In fact, the whole world was watching now. He and his people could do as they pleased; go back home and ignore the case before the court.

"We have to carry something for Qoero, you know Jamana." Jay did not close his mouth immediately and as usual, he sported his eland horns. His gap-teeth could be easily counted. On his left hand was a cigarette and he gave it a quick glance before looking at Jamana's face brightening from the Kalahari rising sun.

"You are right." He nodded.

"Last time they released me and arrested you?" Jay asked. "You never told me the whole story. I thought they had released me because of pressure from Drum and Lillian, but the two never talked about the incident."

"As you know," Jamana said. "They always say we have to identify ourselves during the meetings. I was about to tell them that I'm Jay's friend and before I could finish the sentence some officers pounced on me. The man who was in charge of the meeting told the police to release you, saying they had arrested me and I was you." Jay smiled and Jamana let out a chuckle.

"Many surprises are yet to come," said Jamana, as he turned the key to start the vehicle.

"Yes," Jay agreed. "It is like last time when reporters from international newspapers and TVs thought that I was hiding something from them. But they should wait until Survival International or the gods advise us on the next strategy."

Jay paused. "I thought they would shoot you after they decided to arrest us at the Gate. You and a few others took to your heels."

"It was cloudy," said Jamana. "They could not see who was who." He paused and shook his head as if he had identified a new problem. Jay looked him in the eye but said nothing.

"Did you say Qoero went home alone yesterday?" asked Jamana. "I mean, did she find her way into the reserve?"

Jay did not respond and sighed once again.

"Yes," replied Jay. "Some people have managed to meet their families, some are yet to arrive in the reserve. But I'm not sure what really happened to Qoero. We will learn about what people encountered when we get there."

"What was that thing?" Jamana glanced at Jay.

"You mean at the gate last time?"

"Yes, the day we were arrested."

"It was tear gas; that was why I said it was cloudy and I managed to escape when you and others were arrested."

"And rubber..."

"Yes, rubber bullets."

"Were the women not injured?"

"Only men were tortured. I think children and women could have been choked by the tear gas."

Jay nodded before his eyes strayed into the wilderness. He kept silent. Jamana closed the van's door after inspecting the tyres and nodded satisfactorily.

There were two other men of medium height in the van, one more light skinned than the other who had a sad face. The veins that were visibly protruding around his neck seemed to shake violently as he chewed on some roots. There was no remarkable difference between the two men at the back of the van, except that one was short. His hair too seemed to have been knotted, scattered like the Kalahari Savannah bush veldt itself in Winter. Like his mate, he wore a T-shirt with a tired loose neck, perhaps like the one that Judge Motlhatlhobi, who heard Peolwane's case after he was locked up in prison, wore. Both these two men wore big boots and a disturbing sound could be heard as their feet moved this way and that, almost lost in the big boots.

The van now crossed over a gravel road, away from New Xade. As they came close to the Reserve, Jay, as if he had not wanted to think about it, noticed the presence of the police and wildlife officials more strikingly than before. He did not, could not ignore their presence as was the case in the past. That is before the issue of going back home or finding his invisible people started. He sighed slowly. Something cold slowly crept into Jay's stomach. The thing seemed to wash away the insides, but before he could understand it, Jamana brought the car to a gentle stop. Something like a giggle escaped his lips, before he looked at Jay. Jay himself sighed loudly. The two men at the back of the van sensed danger, and one of them coughed while the other also followed suit. The man who was chewing roots let them drop to the ground. His hands were trembling as he saw eight police officers accompanied by two wildlife officials at the main gate. Jay opened the van's door and stepped outside. He took a step, and the eyes of the security agents, though they were at a distance, paralysed him. Although his other leg was supposed to follow the other, he could not move it. It was a confrontation he had come to know so well, but which he could not avoid until his people were allowed to go back to the reserve.

He had to take precautions. His body froze. His hands were pressed against his sides, unsure. Perhaps he was making a wrong move. His three companions watched him in expectation, their faces registering anxiety, regret perhaps. They looked as though they would flee at any slight word from the security agents. When at last the security agents saw him, they became aware of him, not the van, Jay brought his legs together, glued to the ground. Before he knew what he was doing, his hands were raised high like a pupil who knew the answer to a teacher's question. He was like a hero in a movie surrendering his weapons. Jay looked tired, haunted as he tore at his trousers. When the security agents exchanged glances and words, Jay smiled. He tried to pull himself together, but shook heavily. His body betrayed his will.

Jay's other companions sensed, rather than saw the danger he was in, as they too came out of the van to join him. They followed his actions. Only Jamana had his head held high. The three men's heads were bowed as if searching for traces of wounded wildlife animal that had escaped from a poisoned arrow. Tension filled the atmosphere.

The sun had now risen and it was neither cold nor hot' not even lukewarm. The wind whistled lazily and birds chattered. High in the sky Jamana could see vultures; he stared at them, as if they were study specimens.

A middle aged man detached himself from other security agents and approached Jay and his men. His radio could be heard roaring before he came into clear view. It sounded like the perennial Okavango River flowing from Angola into the northern part of Botswana's Thamalakane River. A mischievous smile occupied his face and walked like a man about to enter the loo due to a running stomach. His hands swayed this way and that, like an old woman broadcasting seeds in a field. A layer of fat seemed to have been plastered on his normal structure. In his left hand he held the small radio and in his right hand a rifle. Though this man wore a dark green suit, Jamana noticed that this was not the same person who had made promises and led to his arrest the day of the last meeting. But he looked familiar.

"I knew you would come," he addressed Jay and dropped his gun, while clutching the radio in the other hand.

"I want us to talk so that you may return," the man added, "or enter the reserve as you please. The authorities have given up and instructed me to come all the way from Gaborone to tell you about this." He raised an eyebrow and smiled.

"I heard some of you have gone inside and some are here assembled nearby. I was not there. I really want us to talk." The man looked at Jay, still maintaining the same smile.

"I do not want to hear that someone has been beaten or eaten by a lion as he tried to return to the reserve alone." The man raised his hand to silence Jay who wanted to say something.

"I want all the foolish officials who have assaulted some of your people to come and learn that there is no more brutality. They must hear this Jay, my brother. They must. Those foolish officers! Have you not heard? The radio announced this morning that your lawyers have withdrawn your case. The authorities have agreed with Survival International that after all, you have rights. In other words, you must be allowed to go back to the CKGR, your ancestral home." He glanced at the radio in his hand. Then he turned to face his officers and raised his hand. Six men came, following his orders.

Jay did not speak, did not move. His friends constantly glanced in his direction as if they were impatiently waiting for his orders.

"You went into the CKGR," the fat layered man's eyes were shining. He rubbed some beads of perspiration with a meaty hand.

"You even allowed some people in. So, I want these foolish officials who beat you up to come close so that you can identify them. Is that right? So that we can now open a case of assault. Not that one which you have launched requesting the High Court to rule that the termination of services and relocation in CKGR is unconstitutional." The fat man addressed Jay. Jay nodded his head as his eyes blinked now and again like a child being hurt by accusation in the elder's eyes rather than his words.

Jamana was looking at the fat man with revived interest now. Even the approaching officers seemed not to disturb him. He tried to raise his head to look at the wild life officials as they neared, but it seemed it was only him and the fat man. He also sensed the presence of his companions as they sighed expectantly. Was this really true? His eyes were betraying him. Jamana's eyes were immobile. He fixed his gaze on the fat man's head. He did not look at the layered build. He was not dreaming. Those widely spaced eyes. Those hollow nostrils. Those cabbage shaped ears. No mistake. Even the voice. Except that now it was a little hoarse because of the layers of fat the owner had accumulated. Jamana's memory was about to serve him well, when abruptly and unexpectedly the officers pounced on him, Jay and his friends. Their hands were handcuffed together at the back. The fat man glanced at Jamana and, as if he saw something that he had forgotten long ago, like one recognizing a childhood lover, his eyes brightened. The anxiety on his face subsided. In its place was a mischievous smile coupled with curiosity.

When their eyes met, the fat man dropped his. Jamana's eyes stayed the way they had been, immobile, curious, bringing back the memory.

But the fat man interrupted Jamana's thoughts. "We shall not hurt you." He directed his words to no one in particular as he led them away. Jay and his men, with the wildlife officials in tow, followed the fat man to a gate where a Land Rover van was parked.

"You went into the CKGR not once, but many times without permission," the fat man said. "I must punish you for breaking the law. You have to spend some days in prison," added the fat man, again not directing his words at anyone in particular.

Jay and his men said nothing but hissed in agony as the handcuffs chafed their hands.

"What more can you say?" The fat man turned around and gave Jay and his men a quick glance, then continued walking towards three Wildlife Department Land Rovers.

"When did we need a permit or license to enter the Reserve?" It was Jamana. He walked close to Jay. His eyes lingered on Jay's lips before they moved to Jay's eyes, questioningly. But Jay was expressionless, indifferent to the question.

"Who talked about licenses?" The fat man turned his head as the four captives were standing next to the Land Rovers. Jay and his men did not answer him. This seemed to irritate the fat man.

"Can't you respond when asked a question?" The fat man's eyes moved from one prisoner to another, his eyes bulging with anger. He hit each man with a baton stick on the head.

"We have relocated your people to a good place." He shook his head as if disagreeing with his own words. "We wanted to provide you with food, resources, give your people a better life, take you away from the animal kingdom and make your people happy and peaceful. But who do we see now disrupting that? A few people indeed. Here, in this country, majority rules. Can't you see that even our leaders are the majority? You might think a parliamentarian is one person but he or she is many people combined into one. That is because the majority voted for him or her. He or she is also our image." He paused for breath and continued.

"That is why when foreigners see our MPs they become jealous of how rich we are; our MPs images reflect how well fed the people of this country are. I heard that you, Jay, told the world that the country is rich but the people are poor. How can people become rich if there are certain individuals like you who want to disrupt the peace that others are

171

enjoying?" With these words, the fat man moved away.

Jamana raised his head as he saw the fat man disappear into one of the vans and drove off. He had not gone far when he brought the van to a stop at the gate. The fat man was now talking to someone on the radio. The person on the other side of the line seemed to be of hard hearing, as the fat man had to shout and repeat words into the small radio which Jamana told Jay was called a walkie-talkie. Jay then understood why the man had used such a device; there was no network, hence the man could not use a cell phone. The wildlife officer who was ordered to keep an eye on Jay and his men ordered them to stand against the fence. Jay stood close to Jamana while the other two men came after Jamana. Jay was standing close to the entrance. He glanced at the gate, the fence and the wall that formed part of the gate. The fence was very high; Jay's eyes met a big sign bearing the words, CKGR, as usual. His eyes moved from the sign post to the fence, the gate and the wall as if he had not noticed their importance before, even since his childhood. Now they were important to him.

Were they not the CKGR itself? Jay sighed hard. He said something in Sesarwa, his native language. His voice was not above a whisper but could be heard by someone a meter away. He moved closer to Jamana.

"What is it that he said?" the wildlife officer on guard asked Jamana ignoring Jay.

But Jamana only showed the wildlife official his bare teeth which his thin lips failed to cover. He said nothing. Then he tried to cover his teeth unsuccessfully. The wildlife officer ordered them to get into the van, which they did without a word. The van drove off, from CKGR to Ghanzi. The captives' own van was left parked at the gate.

"I will come back again," Jay shouted as the van sped off.

# Chapter Twenty One

They wanted to hear about God's wonder - the CKGR - and its residents and their gods. The court was fully packed. Reporters came from all around the world. The witness taking the stand that day was Matsatsing Tswaepe. The three judges had already taken their seats when the witness walked towards the witness box. A court clerk walked towards Tswaepe.

"Raise your hand."

Tswaepe did as he was told with a dejected face.

"Place your other hand on this Bible." Tswaepe screwed his eyes as if the clerk had insulted him. The clerk repeated. "Say what I'm going to say is nothing but the truth." Tswaepe was silent. He glanced at Phoko and Benny for further explanation.

"You must repeat what I say," said the clerk patiently with the voice of an elder to a child despite the fact that he was young enough to be Tswaepe's son. Tswaepe sighed as if he had been chasing a wounded eland.

"Say what I'm going to say is nothing but the truth," said the clerk.

"Say what I'm going to say is nothing but the truth."

"No," said the clerk. "You must not repeat everything that I say."

"No," said Tswaepe. "You must not repeat everything that I say." The court clerk stole a surreptitious glance at the judges.

"For the sake of progress and for the benefit of both parties," said Judge Pamani "let's continue with the cross examination. Or do you have any objection Mr. Benny?"

Benny rose to his feet. "As the court pleases My Lord."

Pamani focused his eyes on Peolwane, a mischievous smile on the lawyer's face. Perhaps the same as the one that Jamana had recognized when they were arrested at the gate. Peolwane's face beamed like neon lights. He stood up. Tswaepe told the court that he wanted to take everything that belonged to him back home. And of course home being the CKGR. He was a middle-aged man but he looked older than his years.

"Mr. Tswaepe, tell the court what happened after you were relocated."

"We just erected huts, but never slept in them," he said. "We slept in the open.

We were waiting for compensation which included money and cattle."

Peolwane nodded as a way of acknowledgement.

"Have you received compensation?"

"Yes."

"Then why do you want to go back if you have received compensation?"

"Because I want to go home," said Tswaepe wiping his mouth with the back of his hand.

"I didn't know that the compensation was meant to stop us from going back home.

Last time when we wanted to go to Mothomelo inside the Reserve we were harassed by the wildlife officers only because we wanted to go home. We will never seek permission to go back home. Never before have we been told that we should seek permission to go home. Does anyone here ask for permission if he wants to go to his farm, home or cattle post? Even if it means breaking the law I will never stop going home. I'm not a visitor. I'm a resident. Only visitors like tourists or someone like you could be asked to produce permits."

"You ceased being a resident the day you were relocated," said Peolwane.

"No," said Tswaepe with a frown as if Peolwane was telling the court a lie. "I was a visitor to the new settlement, New Xade. Just like tourists are visitors to our home, CKGR."

"Why did you hold your wives hostage in the CKGR when they did not want to stay there?"

"I can't remember doing that. I only found that you and others had stolen them."

"Where were you then?" asked Peolwane.

"Away in the bush hunting and mending my traps."

"You said you were left with nothing when relocated, in your affidavit."

"Yes."

"But were you not compensated with cattle and money?"

"Yes I was."

"Then why are you complaining?"

"I'm not complaining; I want to go home."

"That is no longer your residence."

"When did it stop being my home?"

"The moment you received compensation."

Tswaepe paused. He seemed to have been transported to the day he was relocated or the day he found no one at his homestead.

"That compensation was meant to wipe away my tears because I had cried all the way from the CKGR to New Xade and also on my way to this court."

The public gallery burst out laughing. The judges also smiled finding the statement amusing.

As if recalling what he had been instructed to say by the gods, Tswaepe continued speaking even before Peolwane could move to the next question.

"Since the day my wife was loaded in a truck," he continued, "I do not know what has gone into her head."

"Ok, continue," said Peolwane. But Tswaepe paused as though Peolwane had instructed that he should be arrested for breaking the law.

"She has started drinking heavily. She has even started selling the cattle she was given so that she can buy alcohol. I don't even have control over her. I wonder if the people who relocated her have told her that they are better than me and I'm nothing before her eyes."

"So are you asking assistance from the court?"

"No, I want to go home."

It was clear that Tswaepe was a hard nut to crack for Peolwane who paused. Unexpectedly he glanced at the file before him. "That is all we wanted from the witness." Pamani shifted his youthful eyes, which seemed to defy his aging features, to Benny. The British defence lawyer stood up.

"Mr. Tswaepe, was your livestock also loaded in trucks?"

"Yes, but a day after I lodged a complaint while in New Xade."

"You lodged your complaint to whom?"

"To the wildlife officers."

"And what did they tell you?"

"That there was an outbreak of a disease, but I told them that I can cure any disease as I have done that for many years." Benny nodded. Then he glanced at Pamani. "That is all My Lord."

The next witness to take the stand was another applicant relocated from Metsimanong in the CKGR. Peolwane walked toward the witness.

"Now, Mr. Tsimako Beisang, because you stay in the CKGR and your wife stays in New Xade do you still consider her your wife?"

"Perhaps that is what your kind and Emang Basadi encourage," said Beisang. (Emang Basadi was a Non Governmental Organization (NGO) that advocated for the rights of women in the country.)

"Raise your voice please," said Peolwane.

"How can I speak loudly, I'm thirsty. Didn't you cut off water supply to the CKGR? But that is not important to me for now. I want to go home."

"Yes Mr. Beisang, what about Emang Basadi?"

"You should know better. I was saying it is because of organizations like Emang Basadi that my wife does not respect me. She drinks alcohol like the Kalahari sandy soil would drain water after rain..." He paused. Peolwane raised his head from his file and shook his head, while Beisang nodded as if recognising Peolwane.

"I wonder if I'm a citizen of this country," said Beisang his eyes glistening as if they would pop out of his skull. He told the court that he did not know that the CKGR was a part of the country. To him, he explained, it was a land that was independent from the country, a country on its own.

"The law denies us the right to protect our lifestyle. We have been conserving wildlife and nobody has been telling us how to do so. Let me tell you my story. It all happened while I was away from home, I mean Metsimanong. When I arrived from hunting, I found that my seven huts had been demolished. Later, I protested but no one listened. I had then spent the night in the open, because I expected those who had taken my wives and children to bring them back. When they came and emptied the water tank I just looked at them with my face in my hands because they were taking what belonged to them. There was no need to complain."

"But why are you in court then?"

"Because I want my home back."

"Apart from that what else do you want to do?"

"Nothing else but a return to my home only."

"You spent some time at the mines and other places and you call that home?"

"Don't forget that you also spent some time in South Africa practicing law, but you do not call it home." Peolwane was taken aback a little. The truth had shocked him. How did Beisang know about his past? He looked Beisang up and down as if sensing his presence for the first time. He was dumbstruck. Beisang shifted his narrow eyes from Peolwane and addressed the judges.

"From the stories told to me by my father, the CKGR is our home. If I knew that it was state land I wouldn't be in court today. I would have asked father why he had lied to me. But in our culture a father does not tell lies to his son. He told me the truth and I stand by it. I cannot move out of that land because you have discovered ..."

"But diamonds at Orapa and Jwaneng, if that is what you want to tell the court, are national resources shared by the rest of the nation," said Peolwane.

"Stop there," Beisang said. "I wonder how diamonds benefited everybody when people in Ghanzi live in shacks and match box houses."

He paused and looked round.

Peolwane was about to ask another question but stopped midway. He looked at Benny and at the Judges as if for protection. The atmosphere in the court had turned ugly. The two lawyers resembled two powerful countries fighting for oil or a diamond rich colony. For a moment they looked at each other like warring bulls.

"My learned friend is interrupting me and I..."

"How many times should I warn you to behave like officers of the court?" asked Judge Ditiro, the anger at the two lawyers having engulfed him.

"Adjourned. We will come back at two o'clock," he said. The three judges walked into their chambers.

When the court session resumed, Benny did not ask Beisang many questions.

"My Lord, our next witness is a South African ecologist," said Benny. "He was hired by FPK to study maps and also carry out research with a view to finding out whether the residents and the wild animals could co-exist."

"Before you can call the next witness," said Pamani. "I would like to take you back to your argument this morning. You raised a very interesting point."

Benny nodded and his cream teeth were left bare. "Yes My Lord."

"You spoke of the creation of reserves. Why did the British create tribal reserves in this country which are now called districts, Mr. Benny?" asked Pamani.

"Instead of creating a tribal reserve for the Basarwa, they created a game reserve," said Benny. "The British Crown only decided that major tribes would have native reserves."

"OK, let's have the other witness," said Pamani.

The South African ecologist, Ali Anderson, was tall with an athletic body. His face was smooth with eyes that seemed to be on the alert. He told the court that the residents had co-existed with wild animals for many years. They knew when to hunt and which season to allow the animals to breed. According to Anderson, the Basarwa could also teach other would-be hunters which species of wild animals should be left to breed. Those, he said, were classified as endangered species.

Anderson told the court that the Basarwa could gauge the speed of the wild animal by merely studying its paw marks or hoof marks. They could also tell if the wild animal was still young by merely examining its droppings. He said that the Basarwa also depended on wild tubers for water during dry seasons. During summer, Anderson said, they depended on pans and at times some holes found in the trunks of big trees like baobabs. He said the baobab also had a special place in their hearts. They would go to the tree and pray. The court also heard that the Basarwa did not kill wild animals for pleasure. He said they could also mend the broken leg of a wild animal. That on its own, Anderson told the court, showed how responsible and caring the Basarwa were as far as the wild animals were concerned.

"They have special education," continued Anderson. "And if they were to be relocated I'm afraid they wouldn't be able to pass it down to future generations."

"Yes Mr. Anderson, if you could elaborate on the special education," said Judge Pamani.

"Your Honour," said Anderson, "when the Basarwa go into the bush there are stories that they receive there; they share these with their children. They can read the ground just like you and I can read alphabetical letters on a piece of paper. As I said before, they can tell whether a wild animal is male or female or young by merely studying its droppings or tracks on the ground. Apart from that, they have a special bond with wild animals and plants. In other words, they are environmentally conscious."

Judge Pamani nodded to show that he was satisfied with the explanation.

Peolwane licked his pen and tapped his lips with it. "Yes Mr. Anderson but..." At this stage, Benny strained his neck and said something hardly above a whisper. "I'm not talking to you," Peolwane shouted at Benny. Pointing at Anderson, Peolwane said, "I'm talking to him."

"Mr. Peolwane," said Judge Ditiro, who was following the court proceeding with revived interest. "Don't forget that we are in court not in the street."

"But my worship it is my learned friend," said Peolwane, "who annoys me. As an officer of the court he should know better."

"What is it that irritates you?" asked Pamani.

"He was whispering to the witness while I was cross examining him."

"Yes Mr. Benny," said Pamani. "If there is something that..."

"I want the witness to answer not you..." Peolwane's eyes were still fixed on Benny as if he would come to blows.

Turning to Benny, Pamani said, "yes Mr. Benny, you can raise an objection, not whisper."

"Continue, Mr. Peolwane."

"Mr. Anderson, in your research papers, you said that there was alcoholism in the new settlements, right?"

"Yes."

"If someone is drunk," said Peolwane still smarting from his anguish, "does that mean he is an alcoholic?"

"I said, what I saw is that many people were drunk as they had nothing to do except be idle."

"What did they do in CKGR?"

"They hunted and harvested wild berries."

"Mr. Anderson, are you aware that the court went there for a physical inspection?"

"Yes."

"Then what are you telling this court which it did not find there?"

"I'm telling the truth I discovered there."

"Would you agree with what some of the witnesses who told this honourable court that the Basarwa migration was a nuisance to white farmers in Ghanzi and that is why the reserve was created?"

"No."

"What did you mean when you said there is a special bond between the Basarwa and wild animals?"

"That was informed by my discovery as I mingled with the residents. For instance, the elders in the CKGR had asked the youth not to use modern methods of hunting like guns or horses."

"Do you know that the reserve is for wild animals?"

"But the residents were given the place by the British and they kept livestock in Gope and Kikao settlements."

"Moving on, are you saying that if people are relocated they cannot practice their culture?"

"They can't practice the trance dance anymore."

"Why?"

"I think you should know better. Didn't you say you have been to…"

"Mr. Anderson, answer questions, don't ask them."

"Where can they dance; where is the land?" It was as if Anderson did not hear Peolwane's instructions. "The relocation slowed down their lifestyle. In summary, they can't live the way they would want to live. For instance they have stopped dancing; they can't clap or sing. They can't ask for deliverance from their gods."

Peolwane returned to his seat before he glanced at the judges. With a pen suspended above her lips, Brown leaned back in her huge chair as if she would disappear.

"Yes, Mr. Benny."

"My Lady," said Benny. "We would like to request that this matter be postponed because as usual, my clients have insufficient funds."

Without warning, Peolwane shot up. "They are not raising funds," said Peolwane.

"It is only a ploy aimed at assisting the applicants to travel around the country destroying the livelihood and the good name of our beautiful country." Peolwane paused. He sat down.

Benny stood up. "That is all, My Lady." He slumped on his seat like a bundle of firewood being thrown away by a weary traveller. Peolwane rose and adjusted his robes.

Judge Brown's eyes glowed. She straightened up as if she would rise.

"Mr. Peolwane, please sit down. You know the procedures very well. We are not in a bar."

Peolwane reverted to his seat, his pride wounded. He shook and bowed his head, hurt. Benny rose and said there was nothing that he could add.

Brown nodded in Peolwane's direction now. "Yes Sir."

"We oppose any further postponement of this matter. The first applicant and Survival International are the cause of the problems. Otherwise, if it were only other residents we would not be here today shouting at each other. Instead, we would find ways in which we could move forward in nation building." He shook his head. "The Europeans should leave us alone. Have they not done enough harm to Africa already?" asked Peolwane to no one in particular. He sat down still fuming.

The three judges brought their heads together as if in prayer. They murmured something only the walls could testify to.

"This matter has been postponed," said judge Ditiro. "But I must warn the defence that this case does not belong to them but to the applicants. For instance, Mr. Phoko is not also helpful to the case. Instead of guiding his clients he is leading them into what this honourable court warned them against, which is giving interviews to the media. This is the last warning or this court will have no option but to take action. And Jay must attend court sessions instead of telling people false information regarding this case."

At that moment, a man opened the door of the public gallery and entered.

"This court is wasting our time. I want to find my people before it is too late," he said, raising his hands towards the judges' directions.

There was silence except the noise made by people as they shifted from their seats to see who could speak like that. A police officer walked towards the man.

"Don't you dare touch me, unless you do not value your life and the promises that you made to your parents."

The policeman was startled. Never before had an ordinary person talked like that to a policeman. There was silence. Jay walked out of the court, his hands behind his back.

# Chapter Twenty Two

As he arrived home from the court session, he asked himself, "how many times have I been in this court and prison?" At first, he had thought going around the world would make the authorities allow his people to go back home. But where had that led him? From the CKGR to the High Court and then to prison. His thoughts were disturbed by his daughter, Lorato, who brought in eland meat. But his appetite was not for any kind of food. Under normal circumstances, Jay would have eaten the food with passion, especially when it was cooked by Lorato, one of the daughters very close to his heart. But now the CKGR was so close to his heart that he had lost appetite. He missed peace and the only place that he could take refuge in was the CKGR. He ordered Lorato to take back the food and put it away safely.

He then took his wooden stool and sat in an open space, watching the approaches to his home and waiting impatiently. The leaders of the FPK started filling the open space at Jay's home; more and more people kept coming, even those who were not members of the organisation. Jamana and Aron also arrived; the only person missing was Molefe.

"There is no need to tell you why we are here," said Jay. "Some people in the country say I'm a sell-out. But to me there is no problem if I'm selling the truth, even to foreigners. Those who want to buy it will and those who do not want are not forced." He paused. "I know I will have to tell the truth and it will hurt many.

People say that I'm shouting to go back home at the expense of my people; that I want them to be tourist attractions. If that is so, it would be better than slaving at the cattle posts." He paused again waiting for a voice to say he was not telling the truth, but there was none. "I might even get arrested before telling the truth. If I tell the world the truth about why our homes were stolen, it will hurt many. When you look at my people you would be excused if you think they are in a different country, a poor one for that matter. We must go home and the truth can only free us." At that moment there was movement in the crowd. Heads turned toward the movement. Jay also turned and met Molefe's eyes. He had expected fire in these, but instead, there was a smile that resembled triumph.

Jay smiled, unable to hide his curiosity. "Molefe?" Molefe nodded in admiration. "I was delayed. I have a letter from Survival International. You will forgive me for tearing the envelope and seeing the contents. I was impatient to go back home."

The meeting was stopped. Jay was eager to give the letter to the news people. He knew without being told that the message in the letter would shake the leaders. Was this not the message he had been waiting for? The leaders would then ask each other, "why did Jay have to say such things?"

If only they had listened to the cries of his people. After telling the truth, he would know that his people had been voiceless and he had given them a voice. He would be alone. The burden was heavy as he quickened his legs. He wanted to off load it to the newspaper people - the latest strategy by Survival International. He walked away from the meeting. His wives and children wept. Would they see him again?

At first people did not notice. No one did. But they sat up when the story appeared in the local and international newspapers. Survival International had a large following across the world. It told the world of the suffering of the poor and marginalized people. While the leaders dressed in suits, wore diamond watches and drank from bottled water, the people of Kalahari's voices were hushed tones as they were thirsty and hungry, said Survival International. It said the fabric that had kept the Basarwa together had broken. The infection of the virus that is immorality, started when wives and children began knowing that they had equal rights like men.

The organization also spoke of Qoero's death in colourful details such that the picture painted by the words in newspapers was able to catch everybody's eye.

Yes, Qoero is said to have died while on her way to the reserve, allegedly due to dehydration. But there were those who said they understood the impact of the campaign and even Jay's threats to the authorities. Others also argued he had said nothing. But Jay was leaving that to the authorities, to everyone, to understand the cries of his people. But the authorities didn't. It was like Jay had said meaningless things. However, he had created wounds in the minds of local and international millionaires.

The warning by the authorities that the removal of his people from CKGR was not linked to diamonds seemed to have made no impression on him. His words and Survival International were to haunt the authorities and multinational companies even up to this day. In fact, the headlines in the newspapers were to haunt many: *Diamonds Last Forever, Basarwa Do Not.*

And Jay waited for the court to punish him for giving the newspapers interviews as well as sharing with them the contents of the letter from Survival international.

# Chapter Twenty Three

Drum had wanted to be a missionary. He was born in South Africa during the Apartheid era and was a liberal as demonstrated by the way he had helped and associated with black South Africans. He had studied in England, mainly Biblical Studies and Geography. His studies were, in a way, designed to rekindle history, to make peace with the past. He was a descendent of the 1820 British settlers who had settled in present day Port Elizabeth in South Africa. Drum and other liberals believed that the atrocities levelled against blacks had meaning for them. They were not responsible for Apartheid. They were squeezed in the same oppression. Like any other Christian or liberal believers, they did not like what was happening. Drum came to Botswana in 1982, shortly before the first negotiations regarding the relocation began. His main aim was to help the oppressed, to fight on their side, to bring about solutions.

To his surprise, his dream of being a liberal, a missionary, which had nearly vanished when South Africa gained independence in 1994, was revived, resurrected by the relocation of the Basarwa in 2002. The CKGR issue would rekindle his childhood ambition. He would not think of sleep, only the CKGR.

He had once declared in a South African newspaper that he should be taken to Robben Island with black South Africans who were arrested under the Terrorism Act. Even now the CKGR issue gave him sleepless nights. He wanted to go and see for himself if the newspaper reports were true that the Basarwa were tortured by wildlife officials. He also wanted to be tortured, if that indeed had happened. In

South Africa he had tried to make his position known, felt, by the society but only achieved little success. In Botswana, that vision should come true.

In the CKGR there were only white farmers who did not mind or trouble anyone about human rights. Such things were too remote for them. They were only interested in farming. But to Drum, the CKGR relocation had disturbed his inner peace. He did not care, was no longer aware of the dusty Kalahari sandy soil trailing behind him. At first, Drum could not understand his own motives in having agreed to help Jay and his people to go back to CKGR. He would walk through the bush to his car thinking about the plight of Jay and his people. Why had the rights of the Basarwa become so important to him? Let Ditshwanelo fight for the Basarwa alone because that was what it was formed for.

But then he would remember his childhood memories. He had wanted to be a missionary, a liberal. This was the answer to the question that had been troubling him since he had met Jay with Lillian. There was also a time when he had studied history at high school such that he wished he could have been born during the days of well-known missionaries like Robert Moffat and Dr David Livingstone - before Apartheid started in South Africa in 1948. Those were times when the missionaries' work was widely recognized, times when equality was nearly achieved.

But for Apartheid! He had to flee from such practices. But it seemed those apartheid fanatics were always trailing behind him, they did not want to see his childhood dreams accomplished. No, they did not, Drum nodded to no one in particular. They were always after him like a cow on heat. 1985. Yes. Gaborone raids. Drum thought he had failed as a liberal in South Africa and would have fresh start in Botswana. The apartheid government raided Gaborone and about 14 people were killed. They believed Botswana harboured some African National Congress members.

Drum became terribly upset with this incident. He had not known whose side he was on. The ANC members or the then South African Defence Force? But what he knew was that he hated racism. That one he was sure of. Was it not the thing that drove him out of the country, South Africa, into present day Ghanzi, near CKGR? Would his position in the society as a liberal missionary be realized, as he had envisaged? But was he not now in the same land where David Livingstone, one of his role models, had named Lake Nhabe, Lake Ngami? The same land where Sir Charles Warren declared a protectorate in 1885? In a sense, Drum saw himself, as a liberal, a missionary whose duty was to give others protection too - Basarwa rights protection or a Basarwa protectorate. And for no apparent reasonat this reflection, Drum found himself breathing hard, as if he was regretting.

As he sat with Jay on the edge of the stool he had been offered, the confusion he felt concerning his assistance in the case before the Lobatse High Court, nearly gave him away. As Jay raised his head to look at him, Drum retreated to the far end of the stool to conceal his confusion, his fear about the future; but he had to make a final decision. He had to search, examine the depths of his heart. He took the decision as he nodded in Jay's direction. He would help. Drum knew the CKGR very well. He had lived there for 23 years, he said. He had recently been to the High Court on behalf of the Basarwa.

As they sat at the table now, Jay would look at Drum as he spoke but avoid meeting his eyes until the end of each phrase. He would only glance at Drum. This man understood the Basarwa's plight, Jay thought. Jay had never thought that people like Drum would be interested. He thought these type of people saw the Basarwa as half humans, extensions of machines, farm labourers.

At first, Jay had not given Drum any attention. But

Drum's words, his smile, had arrested Jay's attention later. Unlike before when Jay had thought "this one sounds just like the authorities, dresses like them, speaks English like them." But as their conversation unfolded and transformed into a harmonious friendship, a connecting bond, Drum seemed to speak earnestly. Jay wished he had been friendly to Drum before. Not rude at all. Drum understood, he said. It was the order of the world. He was not to blame. Drum talked; Jay observed with humility - not as white man to a Mosarwa, but like a man to his equal. Perhaps that was the quality that he shared with Benny. Unlike his experience at the South African mines where a white man would pat a black labourer on the shoulder with a false smile, Drum was different. Again that wish regarding the relationship between authorities and his people and other citizens was revived. That there had never been this drift, the superior and the inferior, the oppressor and the oppressed. Jay wished that there were people who would consult others before taking final decisions. There would have never been this CKGR issue which had torn the country into factions.

When Drum raised his head from looking at the sand dunes, Jay was gone. He wanted to find out if the police were looking for him after defying the court order not to talk to newspapers. Jay also wanted to be arrested at his home, not in the bush.

# Chapter Twenty Four

"Xhate," a figure called out. "I was coming to see you." The figure approached as Jay stood and interrupted his journey. He did not answer at once or show any surprise. It was clear in the semi darkness that his smile revealed that he had expected the voice.

"Ah Lere," Jay responded at once. "I was on my way to see you before I'm arrested." He approached the old man. Lere was one of the oldest men in the CKGR. As he shook hands with Jay now, he had always found it difficult to call his son by his English name. He called him "Xhate," which meant meat in the Sesarwa language. He was the same old man who had told Jay about the events of the relocation. In fact, he was the one who had always told Jay to let people stay in New Xade and Kaudwane.

"I'm sorry to have spoken against going back home.'"

"It's okay"

"I have to apologize."

"You need not to."

"I have to."

"Why?"

"If people across the sea can recognize us."

"Who are they?"

"The same white people who gave this country independence."

"I don't understand."

"We have been given independence in Switzerland."

"What?"

"Yes Molefe told me about it," the old man's tone carried anger now. "Why do you have to keep it a secret?"

"What secret?"

"That Switzerland has given us independence. We are free to go home."

"I know nothing," Jay said without any note of levity in his voice.

"Where have you been?"

"I have just been released from prison, this morning."

"That has become your new home."

"Yes, until I get my real home back. I was with Drum just now."

That instant, Molefe of the FPK appeared. There was jubilation on his face, which he failed to hide. Lere turned to Molefe after greetings.

"Jay wants to keep the independence a secret thing."

"Secret thing?"

Molefe chuckled. He raised an eyebrow. "Jay, you have been given an award."

"What?"

"Yes, you have been awarded a Livelihood Award."

"By whom?"

"You will have to receive it in Switzerland."

"But you know that we are broke, Molefe." Jay shook his head. "We do not have money for the case."

"I think we will get that money from a foundation in Europe; they will help us."

"I wonder how Jamana would feel," said Jay. "He was telling me that we should withdraw the case and let people stay at the new settlements. You know what, I think it is because when we were arrested last week, the same person who arrested him was his classmate at school in Molepolole, so he feels that he should leave the struggle and find a job. You know that his mother had wanted him to join the wildlife department."

Molefe shrugged his shoulders. He was in deep thought. Old man Lere smiled.

"Let's talk about the Switzerland thing please." Molefe turned his eyes towards him. "It is not a guarantee that we will go back home. It is not independence as you call it."

Lere's eyes were dull. "What is it then?"

"It is a recognition that we want to go back home."

Lere, who had refused to take the seat offered by Jay, moved away. Perhaps it was because he had expected to be told that they were going back home, freely without having to enter the reserve like illegal immigrants entering a country.

As usual, Jay saw the sun emerging from under some of the Moselesele trees far away. It was still clear and one could easily see the silhouette of a figure far away. His two visitors had come so early as if they had heard he was dead. Molefe had also left Jay with some unanswered questions. He resolutely went to the door and stood there for a moment before pulling the handle. The door creaked. Jay looked at it as if to examine any damage he had done. It was as he was inspecting the door that he realized he was not wearing his eland horns. He also noticed the candle that he had used to light the hut and put it out. He remembered that the horns were now his name and identity. When the authorities heard his voice alone they froze; they were even scared to mention his name. They only referred to him as the man with horns. But as for the CKGR residents, his name and voice was a song of joy.

As he left the hut, Jay did not look back at it again. Not even at his shadow, trailing behind him. It was short now. He did not want to look at the hut in case it called him to come back and change his mind. He had resolved to see someone. A person to share his thoughts. Jamana. But was Jamana not about to betray the struggle now?

# Chapter Twenty Five

The distance from Jay's place to Jamana's home in Ghanzi was a long one. But in his current state, Jay saw it as short. This was because on the way, he was trying to reconcile many arguments in his heart. How he was going to convince Jamana not to withdraw from the struggle to go back home? How would he also convince him that indeed the Prince's letter, which he had managed to hide from Drum and Lillian, was something that could help them go back home? As soon as he arrived, the irresistible urge to tell Jamana about the Prince's letter that he had felt on the way to Jamana's place began to desert him. Perhaps it was Jamana who destroyed the mood because as soon as Jay arrived, the other man told him everything. Jay said nothing and listened.

Jamana avoided Jay's eyes.

"Have you heard?"

Without taking his eyes away from Jamana, Jay shook his head. Jamana sneezed twice. "They say she was found dead." Jay was silent. Suddenly his eyes turned from brown to red.

He tried to fight something flowing from his nose with a burning sensation.

"You mean Qoero?" Jay said the very name that Jamana had tried to avoid mentioning, even with his eyes. Had he not looked away when he started talking about her death? There was silence. Jamana raised his head from the ground. "It is all over the newspapers."

Jay nodded and looked away. "You mean Survival

International has already told the world about it?" Jamana said yes, adding that Jay's comments were also in the papers.

A refuse of tyre tube lay before Jamana's feet. His hands were still covered with soot. He had discontinued mending the tyre as soon as he saw Jay approaching his home.

"We could have saved her," Jay said nervously. "We could, Jamana." A twinge of guilt spread over his face. Now he looked away, not because of guilt that he gave the newspapers interviews, but because of shame. "But are we to blame?" Jamana had expected Jay to shrug his shoulders. But Jay nodded again. "We could have traced her until we found her."

Jamana sighed and it was his turn to look away. "But we did not fold our arms. It is the security agents who stopped us. And they did not let us explain."

"That is true."

"She was a courageous old woman."

Jay buried his head in his cupped hands. "Indeed she was." He nearly said perhaps more courageous than any of us but he did not. He still wanted to know Jamana's latest stand regarding the struggle to go back home. What he could only say was, "She traversed such a difficult terrain alone."

"Even the stories of lions did not scare her," agreed Jamana. And then Jamana nodded several times as if Jay had revealed an unexpected truth.

"They say home is where the heart is."

Jay fell silent again. He did not know how to plunge into the subject of his visit. How to start, and where? Especially when the death of an old woman who had been a pillar of strength in resisting relocation had been announced. But was her death not part of the struggle? Jamana's hands were still covered in soot. He nibbled at some eland biltong that Jay had brought without washing hands.

"I heard we have won an award?" Jay asked.

"Yes," said Jamana. "I was about to come and see you but received this bad news and I waited to tell others." Jay nodded several times.

"But tell me Jamana…"

"Yes go ahead."

"Do you think she just died like that?"

"I do not know, Jay"

"I'm not saying you know."

"Then what is it?"

"We have to do something." The trick worked. Jay did not have to ask whether Jamana was going to withdraw from the struggle or not. The answer came voluntarily,

"Yes, the world has to know that there is no turning back in going home."

"Yes, it has to."

"I'm not sure if Qoero died a natural death."

"But who killed her?"

"That is what you and I have to find out."

"Yes, this might be the beginning of the real struggle."

"It is."

"Perhaps they have started doing something to eliminate those who are fighting the struggle."

"We do not have a choice, Jamana, do we?"

Jamana shrugged his shoulders.

Jay raised an eye brow. "Remember that the death of my brother is still a mystery."

Jay was remembering the truck driver loaded with tourists who had helped to arrest him and had shouted 'my God' upon turning Jay's face at the gate.

It later emerged that it was his younger brother. It was reported that he died in prison after he was taken there after he was found guilty of damage to property. This was after he had crushed the truck into the gate. People say that the cracks of the wind screen covered with his blood could still be seen near the CKGR gate.

"That is true," said Jamana now.

Jay scratched his head. "So can't we use these two deaths to renew the struggle?"

"How?"

"You will see."

Suddenly Jay sighed hard. He had temporarily forgotten that Benny had ordered him not to give interviews to newspapers. Should he defy the lawyer's orders just as he was defying the authorities' orders? Should he? The sigh that followed told of the pain of so many years. It was a silent, painful cry that is said to be only associated with sheep. The urge to talk to reporters was so irresistible that he nearly told Jamana to drive to Gaborone.

Jamana nodded again and smiled.

"When are we going to Switzerland?" Jay shrugged.

When he spoke even his voice was detached from the Switzerland trip or the award. "I'm not sure. You will have to look at the letter and check the date." Jay wanted to talk to the reporters again. He had to renew the struggle. Should he tell Jamana that he wanted to talk to newsmen?

But before he could do so Jamana broke into his thoughts. "You know, sometimes my mother gets angry with me. I have never told you that she is the one who wanted me to be a tourist guide after I had completed school."

Now it was Jay's turn not to respond.

So Jamana continued speaking.

"But that would have been a betrayal. Even that day

200

when we were released from prison and then I said I was going to quit the struggle and join that fat man who had ordered that we should be arrested, it was not something that came from my heart. It was like someone was telling me to say that."

Still, Jay said nothing. His eyes were immobile. Jamana, who had spoken all along, looking at the distant buildings of Ghanzi, did not notice this. But he did when he turned to face Jay. Jay was breathing slowly like a puff udder that Jamana once escaped from when it was unlocking its jaws. The cobra's eyes had now shrunk so much that Jamana thought Jay was crying. Perhaps it was the death of Qoero. And Jamana remembered how the old woman had been so close to him and Jay.

At times they would get advice from her on how to renew the struggle to go back home. And to think that she went home alone and died while he and Jay were in Europe! Perhaps if Jay could have seen her before she died, he would not be in this mood. At least she could have said good bye. How many will die like her? Jamana sighed.

"Mosarwa has no voice and when he does," said Jay "it is an omen. We have been denied access to go and bury Qoero. That is why I say that the time to tell the truth is long overdue."

"Jay, in order for you to tell the truth," said Jamana. "You need an oath. Not the media." Jay was silent.

"Why did you say that the person who authorized that we should be handcuffed that day was your school mate? I mean the day of tear gas and rubber bullets," asked Jay as if digging into a different subject.

The answer came straight as though it has always been on Jamana's lips. "Because I wanted to withdraw from the struggle to go home. Again, I thought you would believe me because you do not know my classmates."

Jay nodded and smiled.

"It was my first time to see Peolwane not wearing his court robes like a pastor."

Unexpectedly, Jay rose to his feet. He brushed his behind to remove the tiny soil particles that had stuck on his trouser. He moved away without a word. He wanted to talk to the reporters again. The letter he had hidden from the eyes of Lillian and Drum was from the British Prince, and if he could get support from the British Monarchy, what would stop him from finding his people? But he remembered that he had to prepare for a trip to Switzerland.

# Chapter Twenty Six

In Switzerland where he received an award, he told his audience that he was born in the desert. He told them that it was not a joke that the sun shone everyday, even at night. He said that was why they didn't have proverbs like 'make hay while the sun shines'. They always had sunshine and plenty of it. He was even thinking of selling it to Europeans. Those who heard laughed. But Jay did not join them and their laughter died quickly. He continued with his speech.

"There is not much rain there," he said and continued. "It is arid and it's pale, paler than my skin or it's like your skin. Cactus and trees with no leaves can be found there. But you may wonder why I'm light skinned," he said.

Instead of being black, Jay said, like those in the Niger Delta whose darkness threatened to peel off on their clothes, he would remain light in complexion because his land did not have seasons. It was always dry. He and his people liked the arid conditions. Jay said nobody, except the Basarwa, had shown interest in the desert until now. He still had to carry out research so that when they called him for another award or for an update about the relocation, he would give them correct answers. Who but a fool would want to stay in the desert? Some people in the country had said that long ago, Jay recalled. He said in the CKGR he knew no fears except those from snakes. But he and those wild animals depended on each other for survival. Despite the absence of rain, Jay said they knew nothing like drought.

Any mention of drought would bring laughter to the CKGR's residents. It was a new story to them, a comedy.

"When I grew up there I never knew of any other places." Jay was looking at the heavens as if he wanted his gods to be his witness.

He had to wait for his interpreter.

"I used to think that we were the only people on Earth there in the CKGR. But as I grew up I learnt that there were other people in other parts of this earth. And I learnt that there is what is called a country. You know what, in the olden days our people never had borders. Anyway, let me not waste your time; I'm not a Geography teacher. Yes, later in life, I saw some white people like you. But they never bothered us. They were mostly interested in wild animals. And before I forget, they were really interested in our culture, our dancing. I won't bother counting what our culture involves; you can go there and learn about it. It is the richest in the world and I'm not boasting. Why do you think the British King, Charlie, paid the place a visit? You people are missing a lot. Anyway, let me tell you how it all started."

Jay paused. The room where he received the award was so packed that some people had to sit on the floor, while others were turned away; but still they assembled outside. They wanted to see the man from the desert who was giving the authorities in his country sleepless nights. Some had even expected to find out that the man had schooled in Russia. They were treated to a new dose when he lectured them in his Basarwa languages full of so many clicks that some of them gnashed their teeth in fright thinking the man would bite his lips or tongue. The hall was guarded by more than fifty soldiers. People wanted to see the man with horns. Was this not a fauna? They wondered.

That day Jay as usual was wearing his homemade animal skin coat. That was his suit. It distinguished him from all the guests. Indeed this man was still following his culture, those who managed to get a glimpse of him thought. His companion also had the same attire. What was remarkable about him was that he was a little taller and darker, like the people from the Niger Delta that Jay spoke of. His teeth protruded and they were only held in check by his thin upper lips. As he translated, he kept on placing his hand over his lips as if to protect them from falling. He spoke

English, fluently as if he was born in a family where English was worshipped, speaking the language even better than some Englishmen.

"One day when I was deep under the mine." Jay looked at his audience and they could see the sun shine in his eyes. "My white boss came and told me in Afrikaans that my mother had passed away," he continued. "I asked him where he got that from and he said from a visitor outside. Can you guess whom I found there? None other than my own mother! I fainted. Fate was mocking me. Was it a ghost or my own mother? I was taken to the clinic. Later on my mother came to visit and she told me about the relocation. They were to be relocated from the reserve. That was what she meant when she said she was dead. She was announcing her own death." He paused for impact.

"You know why? In our culture when you move someone from where his ancestors are buried you are in a way taking away his life. We believe in the gods. They are our protectors from danger. Even from our enemies. To us, relocation is something unusual. We like where we are, my mother said, repeating what she told the authorities. But later on she wished she could have agreed to satisfy the hunger and thirst, which trouble her even to this day because there are no resources there."

Jay swallowed and wet his lips then continued.

"The water supply has been cut. I need your help to take my people back home, going back to CKGR," he said.

He wiped away perspiration from his eyes. His audience could feel his pain, as they nodded many times.

"You people, my people are more afraid of the authorities than anything else in this world. They are even afraid of talking in loud voices. They only speak in hushed tones. They don't hunt, in fact there is nothing that they do. When they think of doing something they think they are breaking the law. But whose law? People, I don't want to waste my time here telling you that those laws are not ours."

And with these words, Jay stood up. Those who were there said the man's words were touching. They were piercing like a hot sword. Some of them even told him they couldn't understand how he had remained strong up to now despite reports that he had been tortured and even received death threats. When Jay talked, one could feel as if he was talking straight into one's own heart.

"We are all looking for people like you to love us. And I can see that you can't resist. This award is not for me alone. It is for my people in the CKGR. Let me tell you something full of wonder. The first time I called a meeting to ask people if they were willing to relocate, no one showed up. I thought maybe they had already relocated. But people, guess what? Lend me your ears. After I had climbed a tree to see if indeed there was no one I saw a few people there and there. I went to them. Please remember that this was in the new settlements. They showed me their heels. I thought I did not understand my people. Perhaps it was because I had stayed too long at the mines, I nearly collided with my own sister as I rushed to stop those who were running from the opposite direction. She was also running away from me. There is no trust among the people themselves. Later on when I told them that I was their own son and they recognized me, they cried. All of them. Why do you think I wear this home-made skin jacket?"

Jay was told to stop giving his speech because many people, gathered in the hall, fainted. Some were wailing as if possessed by demons. Hot tears stung their eyes. His suffering reminded them of the historic Jewish concentration camps during Hitler's rule. Jay ended his speech by telling his listeners that he would show the authorities the award as a permit that his people should indeed go back to the CKGR. And he believed that they would agree, especially since the award was from abroad. The judgment on whether to go back to CKGR or not was only a day away, he told his listeners.

# Chapter Twenty Seven

The Basarwa had to seek prophesy about the court judgement. They had to know whether the outcome of the case would mean anything to them, whether they would lose or win it. The medicine men had to talk to the gods and ask them the meaning of the court case for the first time. Why had they forgotten to seek help from their ancestors as Jay had told the courts? But it was not late. The moon sifted through the huge baobab tree like the headlights of a car entering a bush where there are no street or traffic lights. Four men emerged from the beehive mud and grass huts toward the open space.

When they were in the clearing, the moon silhouetted their bodies such that they looked like pictures on a black and white TV screen. Their skins glowed when they reflected the moonlight and they all wore the traditional loincloth called axai. Titae led the group and in both his hands were small sticks of Motsotsojane with which he was readying to make a fire. Three men hovered over him as he sat down. The women had already gathered and made a circle round the men. They sat on their knees and started to clap their hands, singing sacred songs.

Welcome to the sacred dance again.

It had begun. It was in Kikao, not far from the CKGR. How the Prince would have loved to watch it again. But now it was only Benny, the lawyer for the Basarwa. Benny noticed that the fire started to glow in time to the men's shining eyes as they were already on their feet, including Titae. Their feet shuffled the sandy soil reminding Benny how he used to turn up the soil to let air penetrate the roots of a plant during a practical Science lesson at school. It was a sight to behold, especially the dance of the old woman that Jay had introduced to Benny as the mother of the late Hirschfield. Her name was Mmese. Benny also learnt that she was called the mother of the FPK.

This was because her son had formed the organization with Jay. Benny remembered that Jay had told him that Hirschfield's father was a white man. No wonder the man had fallen in love with her. Mmese was tall and her frame was reminiscent of women whom tradition dictated were reserved to bear kings. Her skin was the colour of honey. Benny learnt that Mmese was from Groote Largete in the Kalahari Desert. People said she was aged 75, but she looked younger than that, Benny observed. Her face was smooth as though it had defied the wrinkles that were hidden in her honey skin. But above all it was Mmese's eyes that captivated the observer. They seemed to pop out as if defying her relaxed eyebrows. It was as if they were inviting a man who had stayed long in prison, to bed.

A man had been lying on Mmese's lap like a child with his face turned upside down. She fixed her eyes on the fire, and then back to the man on her lap. She shook her head several times. The four men were still stomping their feet. But now their pace had quickened and they were panting to breathe. "Jay, what has happened," she said. "Don't hide anything from me. I'm your mother. Remember when you and Hirschfield, my son who died from cancer, formed FPK, you gave our people a voice," she said to the man lying on her laps. Jay said nothing except incoherent words.

"We will get the land," continued Mmese now in a sorrowful tone. "But if there is still fear among our people and threats from authorities, there is nothing that will benefit us from it. It would be like getting an empty vessel, a curse."

Titae had now fallen on the sand clutching the ground and groaning. Mmesa put Jay down on the sand and started to shuffle her feet, talking to the ancestors as she did so. She began leaping in and out of the circle touching each of the women on her head. The three men were hovering over Jay now. Mmese faced the sky, and seemed to be fascinated by it. Perhaps it was because now there were many stars in the sky. To her, it was like they were many, perhaps more than before. They sparkled but ominously mocked her. They reminded her of part of the truth that Jay and Survival International claimed and was denied by the authorities. Had they not said that they were relocated because of diamonds? And the sparkling was just the same, though she had never set her eyes on a diamond. By now wetness was streaming from her nose and her spittle flowed to the ground.

At the same time, Jay's groaning increased.

"We will go back home but our people will never be free," she said shaking her head again. "I foresee more danger. The land will no longer be useful to our people even if we win the case."

By now her breathing was in gasps. Hovering over Jay, Mmese placed her hands on his heart and head as if feeling his body temperature. Exhausted, she collapsed on the sand simultaneously with the four men next to Titae and Jay.

# Chapter Twenty Eight

"There is no need to attend court," Jay said.

"Why?"

"Because they fail to say the truth. After all, I have already told the newspapers why we were relocated."

"Give Benny a chance, Jay."

"What chance?" Jay's voice was raised. "How long have we been fighting? Didn't you hear him say that part of the information which deals with the truth is not in the application? You heard him tell the court that. And you told me that a man does not tell lies before a court of law. It would have been better had we cooperated with WIMSA, Ditshwanelo and others and withdraw the case." Jamana did not answer for a moment.

"Remember, Jay," Jamana said at last when he got the opportunity, "that the case does not belong to me, you or any of the lawyers. It belongs to the 241 applicants.

Even the court said that when it dismissed the first application we launched."

"When we went to Gope," Jay said, ignoring Jamana's explanation, "did Benny tell the judges what he had agreed with us? No he didn't. You told me that he even raised an objection when Peolwane told the court that we should travel to Gope in a plane. I would have told the judges the truth myself."

"How many times should I tell you that to tell the truth to judges, you need an oath?"

Again Jay ignored Jamana. "But I could not tell the truth then because I was confused. The journey by a helicopter had made me lose direction. I got lost as if I was not in my home. How can I get lost in a place I grew up in and knew so well even if I were to be awoken from sleep? But that journey. Either something went wrong that day, or it was the way it was planned. You know, it was like I had been dancing the trance dance. I think it was a ploy to deny me the opportunity to tell the truth. The very truth that forced us to go and make an inspection at Gope. How could I lose direction?"

"Oh, you mean that?" said Jamana. "It is called bearing; you lost your bearings that day I remember."

"Whatever it is," Jay said, "why didn't we use a van? I mean even people who have royal blood flowing in their veins like the British Prince always use vans when they come here, though they sleep in planes when they are in England."

"Jay," Jamana said, "those were judges; people who can order someone to be hanged regardless of their status in the society or colour. Remember that people had thought the South African woman would not be touched by the hangman... I mean Marietta Bosch. If they could not only hang a white woman, but also a mother, Jay."

Jay shook his head. A new thought had struck him. He nodded in Jamana's direction before he looked at Molefe.

"We need a new strategy, new companions to help us go home. I agree with Jamana that let's forget about..."

Molefe shook his head. In fact he laughed.

"I still want Ditshwanelo, WIMSA, and..,"

"No you can't say that." Jay's voice had a trace of threat. "These organizations say that they know many things about human rights. But people are hung, people are assaulted. They have never done anything to convince me that they are sincere in what they say they were formed to do. Show me anything that they have done, just like the leaders; they only hold cocktail parties, wasting money and nothing after that. I haven't seen the results..."

Jay's voice trailed off. Perhaps it was the cigarette in his lips or the threat in Molefe's response.

"IsDitshwanelo not the organization that helped those

people from being hanged at the last hour?" asked Molefe, remembering the two Basarwa men who were acquitted after being sentenced to death.

"Yes, but...but" said Jamana now. "We thank the local organizations for the job well done and the assistance that they offered, but we would like to have Survival International alone. We are of the view that these local organizations are the root source of the problem. They are the ones who are stalling our plans to go home." He paused for breath.

"They have diverted attention. Going back home is more serious than protecting a man who has been condemned to death. We did nothing wrong. We never killed anyone and we are not even linked to any murder. These organizations have protected the murderous. Have they escaped the hangman? No. You talk about the two men, yes even a newly born baby would have stopped their execution. These organizations do not care if we go home or not. After all, are their leaders not cattle barons? They want nothing more than seeing us being their herd boys. We need a human rights organization that uses the latest technology, to match those who want to prevent us from going back home. We can't wait to go back home, Molefe you know that."

"But negotiations are the last resort," said Molefe. "I have already written a letter to the authorities so that we can negotiate..."

"You did what?" Jay stood up. His hands were on his waist. Molefe did not answer but instead rose to his feet too.

"We need a voice," said Jay, "that can be heard by the rest of the world."

"But you have failed to go and tell the court the truth. Instead you have been hiding in the FPK office or running around the world like a politician canvassing for support during the general elections," said Molefe.

"Molefe," said Jay now, fuming, "I did not form FPK for nothing, nor did I make things that led us to be in this situation. I formed this organization with Hirschfield because the voices of our people were troubling me. We were the only ones who understood their cries. They sent me so that you and I could take their cries and give them a voice. Do not talk like a child."

With these words Jay walked away and entered the Lobatse High Court. The situation mirrored the time Jay and Jamana had arrived from Britain only to hear from Molefe that the judges were in the CKGR. Now Benny was there but he could not understand the argument between these men. He stood speechless, glued to the ground and waiting for Molefe to explain. Molefe was about to explain but stopped as the courtroom door opened.

"If you don't tell the court the truth, Benny...," Jay said to him, coming out of the courtroom. This did not need to be interpreted as Jay pointed at Benny as he spoke. "... we will turn the court into a circus. And remember what happened to Peolwane. You do not want to come all the way from Britain to be jailed in an African country. That would be lowering the standard of the Queen."

Benny shrugged nervously. "Let's go inside the court," he said to Jamana. "Have you forgotten that this is judgment day? There is nothing more to tell the court." Jamana, Jay, Phoko and Benny walked inside the court.

0-0-0-0-0

He remained on the bench of the Lobatse High Court, unable to rise to his feet. All of a sudden, Benny walked out of the court and shook hands with him. Phoko and Jamana were there as well.

"Though the judges did not say who won," said Benny, taking off his huge black gown, "we scored more points. This means that the people can now go back to the CKGR."

Jay listened. He wanted to shout, jump because of happiness, triumph. In fact he did shout a few words: "Victory, Victory." But only for a moment. As he came out of the Cumberland Hotel a few minutes later where a press conference was held, the memories of his childhood rushed into his mind. Perhaps it was the court judgment that had caused him to forget so soon. To forget that he had saved nothing. And the words of Mmese at the last trance dance...

Like an uncontrolled power of the trance dance, everything appeared blurred to Jay now. Had he been right all along? Perhaps everybody who supported the relocation had been right, perhaps he had been wrong. But his people were happy. And he was happy a few minutes ago inside the court. Now that happiness distilled into something else. A feeling of hollowness, of a man who had failed to save something, a loss. Perhaps there was nothing to have saved after all. Some citizens were happy. Reporters from all over the world had come to share his people's joy with the rest of the world. How good it was to go back home after such a long struggle like Nelson Mandela after prison in 1994.

"We knew that the court would be fair," said one man, nodding his head toward Jay. "After all, you have been right," the man said, now addressing Jay.

The man wept with happiness. He expected the same happy response from Jay. But there was only a look of horror, terror. Jay only registered the old CKGR on his mind, of him and other men following a herd of elands. Or looking for herbs; the children with pot-bellied stomachs playing cheerfully and raindrops beating their naked bodies.

He tried to think of the present moment joining his people in their happiness, their celebrations. Had this not been the happiness they had been waiting for. But he only had the feeling of an old man who had given up on life, negated his dreams, knowing that where he was would be where he would be buried. He wiped away teardrops. It suddenly occurred to him that this was the first time he had shed so many tears since the struggle for the ancestral land, CKGR. And indeed it appeared that he was mourning it.

Still people hung around in groups. They waited for him to come out of the hotel,. into the open. They chatted and shared their happiness with him and his people.

"Tears of joy," said an old woman to another when she saw Jay emerging from the Hotel Conference Room followed by reporters.

"Has he not sacrificed his life for this moment?" asked another.

"Even if it were you, you would have cried. You know joy is a pain on its own at times, especially when you get what you have been fighting for after a long time."

But to Jay, he was not his former self. He felt like a civilized person embracing development. He tried to bring himself to match the ancestral land with this other self, his former self. But he could not. Energy ebbed from his knees, his limbs, his toes, his whole body. He was seized by a spasm of terror. Perhaps by the spirits. He was in a trance. But there were no other Basarwa around the fire clapping their hands for the trance dance. It was a bright morning. There was no darkness which could have made it the right time for the trance dance. In his state of mind, again he saw the CKGR sprawling before him. Now it was full of terror, tear gas, rubber bullets and security agents...

"That place had been the ancestral land once. The trance dance, talking to animals, to the trees had been the core of their life...They were pure, fresh like milk straight from a cow's udder ..." he said to himself and paused.

And again how the words of Judge Brown had been sharp like an enjoyable pain: "Our way of life may be different but it is worthy of respect." Jay had nearly stood up and shook the judge's hand. It was as if he and the judge had known each other, were from the same place, or the same mother even. But where were the authorities so that they could be lectured by one of their own?

"But those who took my people away from there brought the impurities, and the ground on which they were relocated had destroyed them entirely," he also remembered his words to those who were interested in knowing, newspaper people.

Again the newsreel, fresh in his mind, now trailed behind him vaguely as if it were from a far off place-prostitution, alcoholism and... He did not want to hear the word because it conjured up horrifying images of people on the verge of death: hollow eyes, red lips, sagging skin, bones that could virtually be seen. But the seven letters rang in his ears: HIV/AIDS. So this was civilization and development.

He tried to compare the new settlements and the CKGR. There was nothing that he had saved from the CKGR.

"...But Mr. Jay, are you going back to the CKGR?" The reporters were back. "How do you feel after winning the case Mr. Jay?"

He blinked and bowed his head at the same time. It was as if he had lost his voice once again. Perhaps it was drowned by the judges, their final words, their judgment. It was like the judges had announced the death of the CKGR, of his voice, in those papers, unlike when he had seen Benny handling the court papers with care. Jay raised his head and his tears were like the flowing mighty Okavango River. It was as if the judges had pronounced the dangerous Section 203 of the death penalty. The Judges had decided the future of the CKGR, Jay observed with guilt.

They were right and independent in their judgment, some of them being human rights activists themselves. But to Jay, as pangs of guilt pricked him, their words had seemed false, untrue. It was as if they were speaking to themselves. This was despite the live TV cameras and the whole world watching. He realized that the case had been tried in the media more than in the courtroom.

How he, a man brought up in the ways of his people, had failed them. He touched the strings that held together the eland horns around his head. He glanced at them and put them in his pocket in case his mind would be changed by looking at them again. The struggle, after all, had been a dream, an idea in the streets of Gaborone, in the Kalahari Desert, in Britain, Russia, France and United States. He took the last puff from a cigarette and paced towards the van. Without a word, he indicated with his hand to the Gaborone road that they should go at once. Jamana, grasping the situation in that moment, as he had always done, drove off. His protruding teeth registered more sadness than his face.

"I don't know why I didn't realize it," Jamana said. "Jay, we have been misled all along. The real people who have been wrong..." He paused. "...are the British. They practiced separate development by creating this reserve. Just like Apartheid in South Africa."

Jay looked at him with furrows on his face. "But the British parliamentarians were here on a fact finding mission. Why did you not raise the issue? Why didn't you tell me so that I could have asked them? Remember that I have been to South Africa. Independence of that country found me there in 1994 while working at the mines."

"But I have only just realized that Survival International has been using us."

"Why didn't you say so when the campaign started?" Jay asked.

"Because I enjoyed the international trips."

Jay quietly shook his head.

"The glamour that came with it," added Jamana. "Didn't we enjoy, Jay? Almost emulating tourists who come here to take our pictures and sell them to make money. Can't you see the truth which we did not see...?"

Jay had learnt that the best kept secret in CKGR after all, was not the discovery of diamonds by the powerful and corruptible who wanted to come up with a new deadly route in humanity, but his people's ancient simple life style. That was the secret, that was how humankind used to be. And no matter how civilized the leaders were, even to the extent of using modern courts, they will never win a battle against their own ancestors' way of life which Jay's people clung to with a shocking tenacity, even up to this day. The ancestors of the leaders, realizing how their own new generation had betrayed them as far as culture and tradition were concerned, decided to be on the side of Jay's people and his powerful spiritual gods. It was *The Trial of the Gods*.

# Glossary

**Basarwa, singular Mosarwa:** The indigenous people of southern Africa, whose territory spans most areas of South Africa, Zimbabwe, Lesotho, Mozambique, Swaziland, Botswana, Namibia, and Angola, are variously referred to as **Bushmen, San, Sho, Basarwa, Kung,** or **Khwe**. These people were traditionally hunters and gatherers, part of the Khoisan group and are related to the traditionally pastoral Khoikhoi. Starting in the 1950s, and lasting through the 1990s, they switched to farming as a result of government-mandated modernization programs as well as the increased risks of a hunting and gathering lifestyle in the face of technological development. There is a significant linguistic difference between the northern Bushmen living between Okavango (Botswana) and Etosha (Namibia), extending into southern Angola on the one hand and the southern group in the central Kalahari towards the Molopo, who are the last remnant of the extensive San of South Africa.

The Bushmen have provided a wealth of information for fields of anthropology and genetics, even as their lifestyles change. One broad study of African genetic diversity completed in 2009 found the San people were among the five populations with the highest measured levels of genetic diversity among the 121 distinct African populations sampled.

The terms San, Khwe, Sho, Bushmen and Basarwa have all been used to refer to the hunter-gatherer peoples of southern Africa. Each of these terms has a problematic history, as they have been used by outsiders to refer to them, often with pejorative connotations. The individual groups identify by names such as Ju/'hoansi and !Kung (the punctuation characters representing different click consonants), and most call themselves by the term

Bushmen when referring to themselves collectively (Source: Wikipedia)

**Batswana, singular Motswana:** are a Southern African people. The Tswana language belongs to the Bantu group of the Niger-Congo languages. Ethnic Tswana make up about 20% of the population of Botswana; however, they have managed to inject their culture to the majority of the tribes in Botswana. The term Batswana is sometimes used simply to mean citizens of Botswana, supporting the assimilation policy and can include Khoisan people, Whites and Coloureds (Source: Wikipedia)

**WIMSA** - The Working Group of Indigenous Minorities in Southern Africa; Non Governmental Organisation (NGO) that advocates for minority rights in Southern Africa.

**Ditshwanelo-** Centre for human rights: Non Governmental Organisation (NGO) that advocates for changes in laws, policies and practices and tries to raise public awareness of rights and responsibilities in Botswana.

**Chibuku:** a traditional beer recipe made from sorghum and/or maize corn.

**Mogoditshane:** a residential area in Botswana's capital city, Gaborone

**Tsolamosese:** a residential area in Gaborone

**Setswana:** One of the official languages in Botswana apart from English

**Mma Mosadinyana-** a name given to the Queen of Britain by Batswana

**Motsojane-** cross berry